We were falling apart.

We had been falling apart before, but now we were a walking disaster area. And I was captain. Maybe the other kids couldn't see it the way I did. We acted like we were the same old Pinecones, but we weren't. We weren't being funny anymore. We were being pathetic. And I *hated* that. As captain, I had to find some way of pulling this team together.

Look for these and other books
in THE GYMNASTS series:

THE GYMNASTS

#8 CAPTAIN OF THE TEAM

Elizabeth Levy

AN
APPLE
PAPERBACK

SCHOLASTIC INC.
New York Toronto London Auckland Sydney

ISBN 0-590-42820-9

12 11 10 9 8 7 6 5 4 3 2   0 1 2 3/9

Printed in the U.S.A.   28

First Scholastic printing, November 1989

*To the real Big Beef,
and the six captains.*

CAPTAIN OF THE TEAM

Pouting Is Not
a Gymnastics Event

"It's time to get serious again," said Patrick. I groaned. When Patrick says "get serious," he's not fooling. He's my coach at the Evergreen Gymnastics Academy.

"Darlene, no groaning," warned Patrick.

I grinned. I don't have many complaints about Patrick. I've really improved since I started with him. I've been taking gymnastics and ballet lessons since I was six, but I'm not really outstanding. It's a drag because everybody expects me to be a "natural" athlete because of my father. My father is "Big Beef" Broderick. He plays football for the Denver Broncos. He's becoming known as the "wise old man" of the team. He doesn't mind the wise part, but he hates being called "old."

It's funny because, at thirteen, I'm the "old man" on my team, the Pinecones. When we first started out it didn't bother me that I was older than anyone else. The other original Pinecones, Lauren, Cindi, and Jodi, were all just a year or two younger than me, and we got along great. But the two newest Pinecones, Ashley and Ti An, are just nine and eight years old, and both of them already have more natural talent than I do. It's maddening. At the beginning of the summer, when training camp is about to begin, Dad has to face what he calls the "young Turks" who want his job. Now I know how he feels.

Of course, Ashley is more of a young twerp than a young Turk. Ti An's okay, only she's a little shy.

"Why do we have to get so serious?" Jodi asked Patrick. "The Pinecones are great because we've got the best sense of humor of any gymnastics team in Denver. Name me one team that tells better jokes than we do."

I agreed with Jodi. One of the things I love about the Pinecones is that we don't take gymnastics dead seriously. We work hard, but we laugh even harder.

"Unfortunately a gymnastics meet is not the David Letterman show," said Patrick. "You don't

2

score points for being funny. You score points by being consistent."

"I want to be a contestant," said Ti An.

"Consistent, dummy, not contestant. Patrick's not talking about *Wheel of Fortune*," said Ashley.

"I like *Wheel of Fortune*," said Ti An. "I'm good at it."

"I'd like to wheel you out of here," said Ashley.

"I wish Ashley would stop sniping at Ti An," I whispered to Cindi.

Cindi shrugged. "What's new? Ashley snipes at everybody. We just have to snipe back."

"The wheel I'm interested in is your aerial cartwheel," said Patrick. "I want to see those arms and legs looking like spokes on a wheel. I want each of your floor routines to include two aerial cartwheels. It's time we start impressing the judges with our strength."

"I like Jodi's idea of impressing them with our jokes," I said.

"You can put humor into your routine," said Patrick. "But *only* if your routine is solid. Otherwise the judges won't take you seriously."

"What judges?" I asked suspiciously. We had just gotten through a series of meets and we hadn't done very well. "I thought we were going to have a break for a couple of months."

"We have an extra two-meet series set up against the Atomic Amazons," said Patrick. "I want you to win those meets. They're scheduled for the first and third Monday of next month. I decided that you need a couple more meets to sharpen your competitive edge."

"Let's pick an easier team," said Lauren.

"Lauren," said Jodi, giving her a low "two finger." It's the opposite of a high five. "I like that kind of thinking."

"I don't," said Patrick.

The truth was I didn't like that kind of thinking, either. I was getting a little bored with all the predictable jokes about how much better than us the Amazons were.

Patrick clapped his hands. "Let's go to work. I want to see two aerial cartwheels down the mats."

We scrambled up. An aerial cartwheel is a cartwheel with no hands. It takes a lot of strength to whip yourself around doing a cartwheel with no hands.

Ti An went first. Ti An is so tiny. She looks like she's got no muscles at all, but she did it perfectly. She hardly needed Partick's help. Her arms were extended beautifully. She looked like the spokes on a wheel.

"Darlene, you're next," said Patrick.

"I need a spot," I admitted. When I'm not absolutely sure I can do a trick on my own, Patrick helps me by standing ready to guide me with his hands. It's called a "spot," and you can't have a coach spot you in competition.

Aerial cartwheels are hard for me. I'm afraid to do them on my own. I'm always worried I'm going to fall straight on my head. I started my run and did a little hop-skip. I raised my hands over my head as if I were going to dive into a pool, only I knew that underneath me was a hard floor. It might be covered by a three-inch mat, but it would feel hard if I hit it headfirst.

I threw myself into the aerial cartwheel. Luckily Patrick grabbed my hips to give me extra height or I would have had to put my hands down. I needed him. I didn't have enough speed. I sort of got tangled up as I tried to finish.

Patrick was breathing as hard as I was from trying to keep me in the air. "When you're upside down, as you're about to land, keep your eyes on your lead foot so you can put it down right under your nose," said Patrick.

"Darlene's got such a tiny nose, no wonder she has trouble," joked Lauren.

"We're going to be in trouble with the Atomic Amazons if that's the best Darlene can do," said Ashley. "The judges don't allow any spotters on the floor routine."

"Darlene won't need a spot by the time of the

meets," said Patrick. "Ashley, you worry about yourself."

Actually I was worried about myself, and I was worried about the Pinecones. We just didn't seem up for these meets. We were acting like business as usual, and business as usual had turned into stale jokes and dumb sniping.

"I honestly don't see why we have to go against the Atomic Amazons," Ashley complained.

"They have more girls at your level than any other club has," said Patrick. "And Coach Miller and I go way back. Let's not worry about them." Patrick looked at his watch. "Our session's almost over. Let me see you do some stretches and then some conditioning."

We broke into pairs to help each other stretch out. Lauren and I were paired together. We sat on the floor facing each other with our legs stretched out wide, our feet touching. We made a funny pair. My legs were so much longer than Lauren's that she had to put her feet on my calves. We took each other's arms and gently rocked back and forth. It really stretches the inner thighs.

"Coach Darrell Miller just wants to use us for raw meat to feed his cannibals," said Lauren. "They should be called the Atomic Cannibals."

"Lauren, enough," I said. "It's getting old . . . all this talk about losing already. Let's think

6

about beating the Atomic Amazons instead."

"Now *that's* a novel idea," said Lauren. "A science fiction novel, but a novel idea."

"Stop being so defeatist," I said.

"You're sounding like an old crank," said Lauren.

"Well, I *am* old . . . at least older," I said.

"Yeah, but you didn't use to be a crank," she joked.

Lauren just laughed at me, but I was serious. The Pinecones were really depressing me with all their put-down jokes. It's one thing not to take ourselves too seriously, but we were in serious danger of turning into a true joke.

"The Atomic Amazons are the best team on the western slope," said Ashley. "There was even an article about Coach Miller in *USA Gymnastics*."

"I don't think we're ready for two more meets," said Cindi. "I wonder why Patrick agreed to it?"

"Patrick used to work for Coach Miller. Didn't we hear rumors that Coach Miller thought Patrick was too soft?" asked Jodi.

I didn't like the Pinecones sounding negative about Patrick, and I didn't like my teammates spreading rumors. "If Coach Miller is so great, how come Ti An used to be an Atomic Amazon and now she's a Pinecone?" I asked. "That's proof that we're better. Ti An came to us."

Ti An was blushing. She hung her head.

"Actually I came here 'cause Coach Miller made me feel like I wasn't good enough."

"Probably you weren't," muttered Ashley.

"Coach Miller said I was a talented enough gymnast," admitted Ti An. "But I wasn't a fighter."

I lay down with my nose on the mat to start my push-ups.

"Why is she so mean?" Ti An whispered to me. We were doing push-ups right next to each other. I couldn't believe she could talk and do push-ups at the same time.

"Who?" I grunted.

"Ashley," said Ti An.

"Don't let her bother you," I said.

Ti An sniffed. "I won't . . . but . . ."

"Ashley's just jealous," I said.

Ti An stared at her. "Jealous of me?"

I nodded my head. I took a deep breath and did one last push-up. Then I collapsed on the mat. "I hadn't realized it before, but you've fit in with the Pinecones much better than Ashley has."

"I have?" asked Ti An, smiling.

I nodded. I looked over at the other mat. Ashley even did push-ups with a pout.

But as I looked around it seemed all the Pinecones were pouting for one reason or another. It was all so childish. Enough was enough. It made me sick. If only they gave points for pouting, there'd be some advantage to having Ashley on our team. Unfortunately pouting is not a gymnastics event.

2

Life's Not Fair

The next day we worked on vaulting. I hate vaulting. It's my least favorite event, and I think I'm the worst vaulter of the Pinecones.

I was doing a straddle vault. It's a relatively easy vault; you just split your legs as you go over the horse. But if you don't like vaulting, no vault is easy.

Before every gymnastics event you have to salute the judge, and Patrick insists we do it in practice so that it becomes second nature. I raised my right hand to salute Patrick, when suddenly I saw Jodi's mom walk over and tap him on the arm.

Jodi's mom works as a coach at Patrick's gym. Patrick makes sure she doesn't coach Jodi, and that's all to Jodi's liking. Jodi says that when she lived in St. Louis *both* her parents tried to coach her, and it was a giant disaster. Jodi says the only good thing about the divorce was that she got Patrick as a coach and us as her teammates.

I like Jodi. She's a bit of a flake, but I wish I were a little more like her, not afraid of anything. I always have to weigh the pros and cons of *everything* before I can make a decision.

"Patrick, you have a phone call," said Jodi's mom.

"Tell them I'll call them back," said Patrick. "Okay, Darlene. Make this clean."

I saluted Patrick again.

"It's Coach Miller," said Jodi's mom.

Patrick looked annoyed. "I don't care if it's the Queen of England," said Patrick. "I'll call him back."

"I'm sorry," said Jodi's mother. "I wouldn't interrupt you, but he says to tell you that he's on his car phone, and he'll be out of range in fifteen minutes. It's important. He has to talk to you now."

"Sorry, Darlene. We'll get back to your vault in a minute."

"That's okay," I said. I am always glad for an excuse not to vault.

"I don't want you to stand around getting

cold," said Patrick. "Darlene, lead the Pine-cones in some conditioning. Let me see twenty stomach crunches and ten push-ups." Stomach crunches are sit-ups, but you only go up partway. After a few of them you feel like your stomach is being crunched.

Patrick disappeared upstairs into his office. "A car phone!" exclaimed Ashley. "How cool! Coach Miller has a car phone!"

" 'How cool!' " mocked Jodi.

"Come on, guys," I said. "Patrick put me in charge. We're supposed to do twenty stomach crunches and ten push-ups." I lay down on the mats to start the stomach crunches.

Ashley was lost in space, probably daydreaming about car phones. "I'll bet your dad has a car phone, doesn't he?" she asked me.

I hate it when people make a fuss about my dad. I know it's hard not to make a big deal about him. Dad is plenty big, but I always get extra attention just because of him.

I sat up. "Do stomach crunches, Ashley, and stop talking about car phones."

I noticed the other Pinecones weren't taking my orders very seriously, either. Jodi was doing sort of halfhearted stomach crunches, and Lauren was examining a blister on her foot.

"Come on, you guys," I pleaded. "And Ashley,

no, my father doesn't have a car phone. He says they're a menace to the highways. He says he feels safer on the football field than he does around drivers babbling into the phone."

"Mom's been dating a guy with a car phone," said Jodi.

That did it. Everybody stopped stomach crunching to find out whom Jodi's mom was dating. Even me. I love gossip.

"Who is he?" I asked.

Jodi giggled. "You're not going to believe it," she said. She looked around the room to see if her mom was listening. "Barking Barney," she whispered.

"Barking Barney, the pet store owner!" I started laughing. Barking Barney owns a chain of pet stores around Denver, and they have the funniest radio commercials I've ever heard. Barking Barney does them himself. He always starts out with a stupid joke about animals.

I lowered my voice to try to imitate him. " 'It's Barking Barney here . . . with your animal tip of the day. How do you keep a rhinoceros from charging?' "

" 'Take away his credit cards,' " guffawed Lauren. "Barking Barney ran that ad all last month."

"Stop making fun of him," said Jodi, very defensively.

"I'm sorry," I said quickly.

Jodi sulked. I felt bad that I had hurt her feelings.

Patrick came out of his office. He looked like he was in a very foul mood.

"Why are you kids just sitting around?"

I stood up quickly. "We finished our stomach crunches . . . but then . . ." I glanced at Jodi. "Then we just got to talking. . . ."

Patrick shook his head. He looked more angry than I had ever seen him, and it scared me to think he was angry with me.

"I'm sorry . . ." I said quickly.

"You're not going to beat Coach Miller's team by sitting around gossiping," said Patrick.

"It wasn't Darlene's fault," said Cindi. "She tried to get us to work out, but we just forgot. . . ."

Patrick sighed. "All right, let's not waste any more time. Darlene, it was your vault we were working on. Get up and let's get back to it."

"What did Coach Miller want? Did he want to cancel the meets?" asked Lauren, sounding very hopeful.

"No, he's insisting on changing the day and the time. It can't be on Monday because he doesn't like to have meets so close to the weekend."

"His team must have lost," said Jodi.

Patrick laughed.

"Anyhow, the first meet has been changed to Thursday at four P.M."

"Thursday!" I exclaimed.

Everybody looked at me. "That's right," said Cindi. "Darlene never comes to gymnastics on Thursdays."

"What's that, your shopping day?" asked Ashley. I glared at her. Everybody knows that I love clothes and like to shop. I happen to have a terrific fashion sense.

"Come on, even Darlene's not such a compulsive shopper that she has to do it on the same day every week," said Lauren, sticking up for me, sort of. I wasn't sure I liked the "even Darlene."

"Thursday is the day my dad takes me to see my great-grandmother," I said. "She's in a nursing home. She always expects us on Thursdays. One of the reasons we go during the week is that GeeGee says, 'Everybody always goes to nursing homes on Sunday. People go to church and then they get to feeling guilty so they sneak in a quick visit before the football game or shopping in the mall. I've got plenty to keep me busy during the weekend just looking at all the visitors. But during the week, I get lonely.' GeeGee has a way of saying something like that without making you feel guilty. Thursday's the best day for my dad so we go every Thursday."

15

Patrick sighed. I hadn't meant to go on so long, but I wanted him to understand that I didn't miss Thursdays because of some frivolous reason. Patrick ran his hand through his hair, something he always does when he's nervous.

"I'm sorry, Darlene. We can't change the date again. Coach Miller has already made the plans for the judges."

"Why does he always have to get his way?" asked Lauren. The same question I was just thinking.

"Coach Miller has gotten his own way for as long as I've known him; that's just the way it is," said Patrick. "Can you visit your grandmother on another day?"

"It's my great-grandmother," I said. "She's eighty-four. She's planning on living to be a hundred so she can have Willard Scott put her picture on television."

"Maybe you can bring her to the meet," said Patrick.

"She can't see very well," I said.

"I'm sorry," said Patrick. "The dates are set for next Thursday and two weeks after that on a Tuesday. There's nothing I can do to change that."

"I still don't think it's fair," I muttered. "Why should Coach Miller *always* get *his* way?"

"Life isn't fair," said Patrick, clapping me on

the back. "President John F. Kennedy said that."

"I'll bet somebody said it before him," I mumbled.

Patrick laughed hard. And I wasn't even trying to be funny.

"Life isn't fair," repeated Ashley in a singsong voice.

"Ashley, shut up," said Cindi.

"I will not!" taunted Ashley with her hands on her hips.

There we were again; instead of the laughing Pinecones we were turning into the fighting Pinecones, only we weren't fighting the other team, we were fighting each other. It was getting to be a real drag.

3

The Grand Old Lady of the Pinecones

People have funny impressions about what life is like living with a famous person. Sometimes kids at school think I go everywhere in a limousine and that I spend my whole life shopping.

Even the other Pinecones think my life is a lot more glamorous than it is. I got home, tired from gymnastics, and the first thing that greeted me was my baby sister, Deirdre, pointing to her diaper and saying "Poop!"

How's that for glamour! She's fourteen months old, and Mom says Deirdre's way too young to be toilet trained. I say that if you're old enough to say it, you're old enough to use the potty.

"Mom! Dad!" I yelled. "Deirdre stinks."

My other little sister, Debi, who's only four,

picked up the refrain: "Deirdre stinks! Deirdre stinks!"

Dad heard it all the way down in the basement where he was working out in the weight room.

"Darlene," he shouted. "Your mother's out. I'm in the middle of my reps. You change her."

I picked up Deirdre. She really did stink. And she's not exactly light. I wondered why Dad couldn't do weight work picking up Deirdre.

I changed her and carried her down to the weight room to see Dad. He was covered with sweat. One TV reporter keeps saying that Dad must have made a pact with the devil because he doesn't seem to get old. That reporter should only know how hard Dad has to work to keep in shape. He says he never used to have to work so hard, and that he knows he's going to have to retire soon. But he keeps giving himself one more year.

"Is Debi watching *Sesame Street*?" Dad asked.

"Yeah. Are you baby-sitting?" I asked.

Dad grinned at me. "Don't tell your mom I parked them in front of the television," he said. "I was supposed to be having quality time with your two little sisters, but a little quality time with the two tiny Ds goes a long way."

Dad picked up Deirdre and held her high over his head. "How's my clean little munchkin?" He tickled Deirdre's tummy and made her giggle.

I curled up on the couch. Dad put Deirdre in her portable playpen and got a towel and dried himself off.

"So how's the gymnast?" he asked. He pointed to the weights. "Do you want to do a little weight work — a few reps? I'd like to see you beat the Atomic Amazons."

"Dad," I groaned. "I did about fifty stomach crunches today, and twenty push-ups. That's enough. Besides, the way we're acting, nothing's going to help us. And on top of everything else, dumb Coach Miller changed the date of the meet to a Thursday. I'll have to miss going to see GeeGee."

"GeeGee will understand if we put it off one day. What do you mean, 'the way we're acting'? What's wrong with the Pinecones?"

"Nothing," I muttered.

"Let's go upstairs and I'll start dinner, and you can tell me what's really eating you while I make you something to eat."

I followed him into the kitchen. Dad and I are both good cooks, much better than Mom. Mom's a model, and lately her career's been soaring. She says that suddenly there's a big call for models with a "mature look."

Dad threw a couple of onions at me. "Here, this will give you something real to cry about," he said.

"I wasn't crying," I objected.

"I know," said Dad. "But you seem a little down. What *did* you mean that nothing would help your team? That doesn't sound like you."

"Lately none of the Pinecones seem to think we can really win. We spend all the time making dumb jokes and sniping at each other when Patrick isn't watching us. It's getting boring. Sometimes I wish I could just learn new tricks and never compete." I rubbed my eyes. Chopping onions really makes me cry.

"You'd get even more bored," said Dad. "Sports without competition would get dull."

"Easy for you to say," I said. "You love winning. And you win. We've been losing lately, even to teams that aren't as good as the Amazons."

"I've lost my share, too," said Dad. "But the game itself is never boring. Depressing maybe, but not boring. It's the only thing that makes all the hard work worth it."

"Thank you very much for that sports lecture," I said sarcastically. "It's a thrill to be sharing a room with a living legend."

I guess I was a little more sarcastic than I expected. It's funny . . . I'm almost never sarcastic, except with my dad.

Dad stopped chopping the tomatoes. "Hey, Darlene, I'm sorry."

I shrugged. I wasn't sure what was wrong. I

hadn't even been in that bad a mood when I left gymnastics, but now the idea of gearing up for two meets with the Atomic Amazons just depressed me.

"Maybe I'm getting too old for gymnastics," I said.

Dad laughed. "Thirteen. I wish I were thirteen."

"We're not talking about football here, Dad," I said. "Thirteen *is* old for gymnastics. I'm the oldest of the Pinecones. Ashley and Ti An are only in third grade. But Ashley's started picking on Ti An. They used to be friends. And Lauren, Cindi, and Jodi say they're not ready for a meet. Patrick wants us to get serious, but nobody's in the mood."

"They need your leadership," said Dad. "I'm the grand old man of the Broncos. You can be the grand old lady of the Pinecones."

"Some leader," I snorted. "Patrick asked me to lead a few simple conditioning exercises, and we wound up gossiping about Barking Barney."

"What about Barking Barney?" Dad asked.

I smiled. Even Dad was more interested in gossip than hearing about the Pinecones' problems. "He's dating Jodi's mom," I said. "He's got a car phone."

"So he can bark to his puppies on the road?" asked Dad.

"Forget about Barking Barney. You're as juvenile as the Pinecones and they're plenty juvenile."

"You really are upset about this, aren't you?"

I nodded. "It's just that everything about gymnastics seems so stale. The Pinecones are stale. For goodness' sake, the Pinecones are even beginning to complain about Patrick, saying that he's not really as good as Coach Miller. And I *know* Patrick's the greatest."

"You'd better try to do something to stem the damage."

"Coach Miller is the problem. He is *so* rigid. I think he's driving Patrick nuts. Coach Miller *can't* have the meet on Monday. It's too close to the weekend. Whatever Coach Miller wants, Coach Miller gets."

"It sounds like Coach Miller's playing mind games with our friend Patrick," said Dad.

"Everybody says that Coach Miller is the best coach on the western slope. He's got the reputation for being the toughest and the best."

Dad's eyebrows went up to the ceiling. "Everybody!" he said. Dad hates the word "everybody." I can never get away with telling him "Everybody is allowed to stay up till midnight," or "Everybody is wearing ripped jeans."

"Well, if 'everybody' thinks Coach Miller is the best, and you think Patrick's the greatest, somebody's wrong," said Dad.

23

"Everybody's wrong," I said. I grinned. Dad had got me with that one, I had to admit.

"You know, Darlene, some coaches are bullies. Lots of people think that being a coach means being tough. My best coaches haven't been the toughest, but the smartest or the fairest."

"Patrick's smart *and* fair," I said.

"Then if you think that, it's your job to remind the other Pinecones of it. You're older. You've got to remind the Pinecones of what a good thing they've got in Patrick. Remind them of what they've got in each other. The Pinecones started out with a lot of spirit. It's your job to make sure they don't lose it."

"My job!" I exclaimed. "I don't want to tell the other kids what to think."

"Since you're the oldest on the team, you should be a leader."

"I'm not a leader. On the Pinecones we're all equals."

Dad shook his head. "I've never seen a team yet where everybody's equal."

"You're wrong, Dad. You're wrong," I argued. I wiped my nose. I was getting sick of cutting onions. I also didn't like what Dad was saying. I didn't like it because I was worried he might be right.

Mean as a Pig
and Twice as Nasty

It was the Wednesday before our meet. "There's something I want to talk to you about after practice," Patrick announced.

"Uh-oh," said Lauren. "When a grown-up says 'There's something I want to talk to you about,' it's usually bad news."

"Maybe it means we're calling off the meet against the Amazons," said Jodi.

"No," Patrick snapped. "It means I'm disturbed about this team's attitude. Now, let's put in a good practice. I want us to be sharp."

Lauren started to hum. "I think you've got B flat, Lauren," I said.

Patrick looked annoyed. "Enough jokes, girls,"

he said. "Let's see your routine on the uneven bars."

"Darlene hardly ever makes jokes," said Lauren, defending me.

"Thanks a bunch," I said.

Patrick stood under the uneven bars. The bars are my second least favorite event. I'm so tall that my feet scrape when I'm on the lower bar. But I swung up, getting a good rhythm going.

Being good on the uneven bars is like swinging on a tree branch or on the jungle gym on the playground. Your hands have to be able to both grip and slip in order to move. Unfortunately I had a blister on top of one of my old calluses, and every slip hurt. When we tear a blister over a callus in gymnastics, we call it a rip, and it hurts like anything.

I cast off for my swing to the high bar, but I missed. I hadn't swung fast enough. I stood up on the lower bar and looked at my hands. I had ripped open one of my calluses. They were already bright red with drops of blood. I licked my palm.

"You okay?" Patrick asked.

"It hurts," I said.

"Come on down," he said. "Let me take a look at it."

I jumped down, not wanting to show how relieved I was not to have to finish my routine.

Patrick looked at my palm. "It looks pretty bad. Go put some ice on it."

I ran out to the parents' lounge where Patrick keeps a freezer full of ice cubes and ice packs.

I put an ice cube on my palm. It stung.

I noticed that Becky was lying on one of the couches, icing her ankle. Becky is my age, but she's in a more advanced group, thank goodness. As my great-grandmother would say, Becky is mean as a pig and twice as nasty. Too bad she has to be such a good gymnast. Naturally Becky was the gymnast whom Ashley admired the most.

"Are you hurt, too?" I asked.

"It's my darned ankle," she said. "Every once in a while it gives out on me."

I could remember when Becky first hurt her ankle. She fell trying to learn the Eagle, a trick on the uneven bars that I still can't do.

"I hope it's okay in time for the meet," I said. Becky picked up the ice pack and threw it on the floor, making a puddle. She stood up.

"It'd *better* be okay for the meet. No way will I miss that. I don't care if I have to go taped up to my armpits. I'll be there."

I have to say one thing for Becky. She is a competitor. She really thrives on competition. Becky never backed away from a fight. In fact, she started most of them.

"I suppose the Pinecones are going to be as pathetic as ever," said Becky.

I blinked. I hated hearing Becky talk like that. It just galled me.

"Becky, we try just as hard as you do. Just because we don't always win, or we're not as good as you, you don't have to put us down all the time."

Becky looked at me with disgust. "Stop whining," she said. "Listen to yourself. You're the living proof of just how pathetic the Pinecones are."

"Whining? Pathetic?" It made me sick to hear those words coming out of Becky.

"Well, just listen to yourself. You talk about 'trying' and 'wanting' to win. But a real champion doesn't try. A real champion just does it."

She got a new ice pack out of the refrigerator and wrapped it around her leg. I was trying to think of something to say back to Becky when Cindi came into the lounge, holding her right hand by the wrist.

"Did you hurt yourself, too?" I asked.

"I ripped," she said. I looked down at her palm. She had reopened one of her blisters, and it was oozing blood.

Cindi and I compared palms. "Your rip is the size of a pickle on a McDonald's hamburger," said Cindi. "Mine is just the size of a little dab of relish."

"Yuk," said Becky. "You are both disgusting."

"Thanks for the sympathy," said Cindi. "Patrick wanted me to get you, Darlene. It's time for a Pinecone meeting."

I got Cindi an ice pack.

"Well, I hope he finds a way to put some backbone into the Pinecones," Becky said.

"I'd like to put a bone in her throat," whispered Cindi. I hooked my arm through hers, and we walked out to Patrick's meeting.

The rest of the Pinecones were sitting on a mat. Patrick had one foot up on a bench.

"How's your rip?" he asked.

I shrugged my shoulders. "It's okay," I said.

"Do you think you'll be okay for the meet tomorrow?" asked Ti An.

Dad had said that I was older and if I saw something wrong it was up to me to do something about it. Becky had said we were pathetic and whiners. Becky's words just popped out of my mouth. "I'll be at that meet tomorrow even if they have to tape me up to the armpits," I said. I was glad Becky wasn't around to overhear me quoting her.

Patrick nodded his head enthusiastically. "That's the spirit I want from my Pinecones," he said.

"What are we going to do tomorrow?" I shouted. "Win!" I yelled, but none of the other

Pinecones piped up. "Come on, guys," I said. "What are we going to do tomorrow?"

This time Cindi said "Win" with me, but without much energy in her voice.

Gradually I got the other Pinecones to chime in, but to tell the truth, I don't think we sounded as if we meant it.

5

Seeds of Doubt

Coach Miller is one scary man. Amazons are supposed to be woman warriors from ancient Greece who would rather die in battle than give up. Coach Miller treats a gymnastics meet more like a war than a competition. You could tell the atmosphere was serious right from the beginning.

I had actually managed to do two aerial cartwheels without Patrick spotting me during my warm-ups on the floor exercise. Now if only I could do them when it counted. But I felt hopeful. I was sure we really had a chance.

I finished my warm-ups on floor and got ready to warm-up on bars. Patrick refuses to spot us during the warm-ups for a meet. He says it gives the judges the impression that we aren't really prepared or confident.

Lauren and Cindi were waiting for the Amazons to finish on the bars. The next Amazon up was a little girl. She looked about Ti An's age, and she wore her hair in pigtails. She still had a little bit of baby fat around her tummy.

Coach Miller watched but he didn't say anything encouraging. In fact, he didn't move at all. She jumped on the springboard and grabbed the bar. Ordinarily the coach or someone would move the board out of her way, but Coach Miller just stood there with his hands in his pockets.

There wasn't another Atomic Amazon around so I moved the springboard out of the way for her.

Coach Miller didn't even mumble a thanks. The girl was very tense. She tried to swing up to the high bar, but she missed and fell off. She pouted and looked like she wanted to cry. Coach Miller just frowned even more. The girl managed to get back on the bars without the springboard, but her routine wasn't very good.

I smiled a little to myself. If she was that shaky just in the warm-ups, we'd beat her easily.

The girl came to pick up the springboard, which was next to me. I kind of felt sorry for her, so I said, "Don't worry, you'll do better in the meet." I knew she was my competition, but she looked so miserable.

"We're not allowed to talk to you," she whispered. "But thanks. . . ."

"What class are you in?" I asked her.

"IVA," she said.

"Me, too," I told her.

She looked around guiltily as if she was going to get in trouble for talking to me. I felt like we were in a war movie and I was the enemy. Dad is friends with lots of men on other teams. He says that some coaches and owners don't like their players to "fraternize" with players from other teams, but he thinks such rules are stupid. "Who do I have more in common with?" he asks. "Other offensive linemen or the owners, the guys in gray suits?"

I wanted to tell this girl to lighten up, but suddenly Coach Miller was definitely paying attention to her.

"Hilary!" he shouted. "What are you doing?"

"Picking up the springboard," said Hilary quickly. The springboards are heavy, and Hilary was such a little thing, it was hard for her to lift it. She dragged it along the mats.

"Pick it up," snapped Coach Miller. "You looked like a marshmallow on the uneven bars. Are you too weak to even carry a springboard?"

Hilary turned bright red. She looked like she wanted to cry. I'd hate it if Patrick was that harsh with us. Patrick sometimes gets mad at us, but he's never sarcastic or mean. Listening to Coach Miller gave me an idea of what Becky would be like as a coach.

Coach Miller crossed his arms over his chest. Hilary struggled to pick up the springboard. She had to kind of bump it along with her thighs. She walked over to him with her head down.

"Did you hear the way he talked to her?" Lauren asked. "I don't think I'd want to be an Amazon for anything," she said.

Cindi watched the next Atomic Amazon warm up. "I don't know," she said. "They're pretty good."

We looked around for Patrick. He was watching Ti An complete her routine on the beam. He waved to us to come over. Ti An performed flawlessly.

"Gather up the other Pinecones," said Patrick. "I want to talk to you all."

Ashley and Jodi were just finishing their floor exercise warm-up. Jodi pulled on her sweatshirt so she wouldn't cool down. Underneath her sweatshirt, she had shrugged off the sleeves of her leotard and pulled it down to the waist so she'd be more comfortable. The sleeves of her leotard hung out like two tails from her sweat-shirt.

"Don't do that," hissed Ashley. "It looks sloppy."

"What are you? My fashion consultant?" snapped Jodi.

"None of the Atomic Amazons put on sweat-shirts," complained Ashley. "They always look nice and neat."

Jodi rolled her eyes. "Darlene," she said to me. "You're the one with taste. Don't I look cool?"

The truth was that Jodi did look sloppy. But I wasn't going to put down my friend in front of Ashley. I kept my mouth shut. "Come on, you two," I said. "Patrick wants to talk to us."

We walked across the gym, steering clear of the mats for the floor exercises where the Atomic Amazons were working out.

Coach Miller didn't have any qualms about spotting his athletes. I couldn't believe it. That little girl Hilary did a back flip from a back handspring. Sure, she needed help from Coach Miller, but none of us Pinecones could do that. Even Becky didn't do that move in competition.

Boy, was it impressive!

Hilary and Coach Miller held a whispered con-ference. Coach Miller gestured wildly with his hands. It looked as if Hilary wanted to do that trick in competition and Coach Miller was trying to talk her out of it. She hadn't seemed that good on the uneven bars, but she sure must be a great tumbler. If she was good enough to even *think* about doing a back flip from a back handspring, she was way out of our league. And yet she had told me she was Class IVA.

I shook my head. "Did you see that little Amazon?" I exclaimed to Patrick. "She almost did a back flip. Unbelievable! She said she was in our class, but if she can do that she should be competing against Becky."

"Yeah, Patrick," complained Jodi. "It's unfair."

Patrick frowned. He stood up and looked across the gym at Coach Miller. "She's not that good. . . . That's just a trick that Coach Miller likes to use," said Patrick. He sounded disgusted.

"Huh? How could it be a trick?" I asked. "I saw it with my own eyes."

"It was an illusion, believe me," said Patrick. "She can't do that move without a heavy spot from Darrell. It's just one of his little games he likes to use to intimidate the opposition. I promise you there was never any question of her trying that trick in competition. It was a show he did just for your benefit to plant seeds of doubt in your mind. Your job is to weed out those seeds of doubt."

36

"It's a proven fact that seeds of doubt plant defeat," said Lauren.

"You're right, Lauren," said Patrick. He smiled. "And it almost rhymes. Now look, girls, you are every bit as good as your competition. I want you to go out there and perform with confidence. Now obviously confidence is not something you go out and buy at the supermarket or pizza parlor. It comes from inside. But the work we've been doing day in and day out, that's taught you confidence. Now all you have to do is use it."

Patrick didn't sound like himself. He sounded kind of formal and uptight. I wondered if Coach Miller's little games were getting to him. The truth was — they were getting to me.

Patrick put his hand out into the middle of our circle. We all put our palms on top of his to give us confidence. I put my hand on top of his. Patrick's hand was big and warm. I pretended it was a confidence fountain, and I tried to pass it on to Jodi, Lauren, Cindi, and Ti An and, yes, even to Ashley. Ashley may be a twerp, but she was a Pinecone and we were a team. Maybe Coach Miller's tricks wouldn't work on us if we just had enough confidence.

6

In the Middle of a Grudge Match

"Okay, guys, go for it," I said as we broke from the huddle.

Becky threw me a dirty look. She was toweling off from her warm-ups. "Always the cheerleader," she said.

"What's wrong with cheering my team on?" I asked her.

"It's so amateur," said Becky. "Watch the Amazons, they're always cool."

"I don't want to be cool. I want my team to win," I said.

"The Pinecones don't need a cheerleader, they need a transfusion," said Becky.

"Well, a cheerleader is what they've got! Let's go Pinecones!" I yelled.

Becky just gave me a dirty look. I didn't care.

The meet began. The Atomic Amazons were first up on the beam. The first Atomic Amazon finished her routine without a mistake, and her teammates didn't shriek or jump up and hug her. Instead, they all nodded and clapped their hands. Even the clapping seemed staged. They did about three claps and then put their hands down.

They repeated that routine for the next two gymnasts. It felt more like a boring school assembly than a gymnastics meet.

Then suddenly a judge gave one of the Atomic Amazons a low score. Now the Atomic Amazons came alive. They stood up and started booing. Until then they had acted more like robots than fans.

Patrick would never allow us to boo a judge, but Coach Miller just folded his arms and glared across the floor at the judge.

The head judge took the microphone. "Would the home team please settle down?" she said.

The judge who had given the Amazon the low score had turned crimson.

Finally it was our turn. Cindi was the first Pinecone on the beam. Normally Patrick would start Lauren or Ti An, somebody who's not as good as Cindi. But he had decided on a different tactic. He wanted to start one of our better gymnasts, to give the judges the impression that *all* the Pinecones were as good as Cindi.

"Coach Miller isn't the only one who can try a few tricks," Patrick had told us.

Cindi did a great mount. She looked like she was rock steady. I held my breath as she did her first hard move, a front walkover, but she didn't wobble once. Talk about confidence. She acted like she owned the beam.

But just when she was making a simple half-turn, Cindi slipped and fell. She didn't even try to catch herself. I could see her face turn red under her strawberry-blonde hair.

She bit her lip and remounted, but her concentration was shot. She fell two more times before the routine was over.

She looked really depressed. "So much for Patrick's trick," muttered Ashley. "We shouldn't have started Cindi."

"Stop second-guessing Patrick," I snapped. I stood up and cheered Cindi. I waved to the other Pinecones to stand up, too. We'd teach those Atomic Amazons something about team spirit.

Cindi got a low score, but her score would be thrown out if the rest of us did well.

Fat chance. Ti An was a disaster. This wasn't the first time this had happened to her. She just totally fell apart.

"Uh-oh," said Lauren, as she watched Ti An fall for the fifth time.

"Uh-oh is right," said Ashley. "*Quel* disaster!"

I sighed. I hated to admit that Ashley was correct about anything, but "*quel* disaster" summed it up.

Finally it was my turn. Beam is my best event. I did okay. Not spectacularly, but okay. I didn't fall off, but I didn't have any pizzazz. Patrick always tells us to "show" our routines, not just do them. I was just doing it.

I got the highest score of the Pinecones, but the judge who had been booed gave me a much lower score than she had given any of the Amazons. I was surprised, but there was nothing I could do. Three Amazons scored higher than me so already I was out of it for a medal, and that was on my best event.

But the real disaster was on the uneven bars. I was a little worried because of my rip. When you have a rip on your palm you can't grip the uneven bars. I started easy, with a back hip-circle mount. Patrick always tells us to think, "step, kick, and chin." I grabbed the bar, took a step, and kicked at the same time, pulling my chin toward the bar so that my hips circled it.

But my hands screamed with pain.

As I circled the bar I tried to lift my weight off

my hands. With my hands on the lower bar I straddled the bar, one leg in front and one leg in back. I circled the bar, but my hands were hurting. I let go to grab for the high bar, but I didn't have enough momentum. I fell down hard on my hip on the mats.

I had tears in my eyes. I stood up and looked down at the tape on my hands.

I knew I had only thirty seconds to remount. I squared my shoulders and grabbed the bar again, but this time I slipped just making my mount.

My hands were really aching, and already I had automatically gotten two .5 deductions. I licked my lips and grabbed the bar a third time, but I couldn't get a good grip. I shoveled myself onto the bars, but then I fell again as I tried to just do a simple step rise to the high bar.

Patrick signaled to the judge that he wanted to see if I was all right.

"My rip is screaming," I said through gritted teeth, "but I'm okay."

Patrick examined my palm. You could see it was bleeding a little under the tape. "Don't continue," said Patrick. "I don't want you to get hurt."

Patrick went over to the judges and told them I was dropping out of the uneven-bar exercise.

I went to sit down. The other Pinecones jumped up to console me. Cindi patted me on the back. Lauren gave me a hug.

I could see the Atomic Amazons tittering among themselves. They made me so mad. Jodi gave the Atomic Amazons a filthy look.

"Sorry, guys," I muttered to the Pinecones. "I couldn't help myself."

"Of course you couldn't," said Lauren loyally.

"The rest of you are just going to have to make up for me," I said. "We aren't beat yet."

Ti An did even worse on the uneven bars than she did on the beam. She was just having one of those days where nothing was going right.

Jodi started out great. Her mount was breathtaking, but maybe that was the problem. She didn't seem to have any breath left for the rest of her routine. She fumbled getting to the high bar, and she had to take more than twenty seconds to gather herself together.

Cindi was the last one up. She's best on the uneven bars. "Does your rip hurt you?" I asked.

She nodded. "But it was never as bad as yours," she said.

"Good luck! Knock 'em dead!" I said to her.

Cindi did a mount every bit as beautiful as Jodi's. She rested on the lower bar and grabbed the high bar. She pulled herself up with a beautiful kip (a kip looks like a diver doing a pike except that it defies gravity and goes up instead of down) to the high bar.

She was really swinging. I knew her hands must be hurting, but she finished her routine with a flourish.

I jumped up and hugged her. But the judge who had scored me so poorly also gave Cindi a low score. It wasn't fair!

Cindi was the last gymnast on the uneven bars, and there was a little break in the action as the Atomic Amazons set up the mats for the floor exercise.

Cindi and I sat on a bench examining the tape over our rips. Coach Miller came by and extended his hand to Cindi. "Now *you* are a fighter," said Coach Miller.

Cindi looked a little shocked, but she was too polite to refuse his hand. "I see you had a rip, but you didn't quit," said Coach Miller. He didn't even look at me. It was like I was a piece of dirt. He might as well have called me a quitter to my face. I felt like sinking into the floor. I wished the mats underneath my feet would have just opened up and buried me.

Patrick overheard Coach Miller. "Please don't comment on my gymnast's performance," he said.

"What's the matter, Patrick?" asked Coach

Miller. "Are you afraid that I'll steal the one good gymnast you've got in this group?"

Patrick looked as angry as I've ever seen him. "Darrell, I do not have *one* good gymnast, I've got a team of them. And I didn't have to try to intimidate a judge or use any other dirty tricks. And I don't like you trying to recruit one of my girls."

Coach Miller grabbed Patrick's arm. "If we want to talk about recruiting," he whispered, "let's talk about Ti An."

"Ti An came to me because she couldn't take your bullying," said Patrick. He walked away.

Cindi and I stared at each other. We couldn't believe how angry Patrick had sounded.

"I think we're in the middle of a grudge match," I said to Cindi.

"Yeah," Cindi agreed. "Unfortunately we're losing."

"Only on points," I said, as I thought about the way Patrick had stood up for me. "Only on points."

7

Give It Up?

We looked like a bunch of whipped puppies as we filed into the dressing room after the meet. The dressing rooms at Amazon's Gymnastic Center are incredibly glamorous, at least compared to our cinder block walls. The Atomic Amazons share their space with a downtown health club, and all the lighting is discreet pink to make the ladies look pretty.

All the pretty pink couldn't do anything for the Pinecones' mood. The meet had been a blowout. We didn't place in one event. Naturally Becky's group had done terrifically. Becky won a silver ribbon on beam, a gold on the uneven bars, and she had come in second in the all-around. Her team had beaten the Amazons on the uneven bars and had pulled much closer than we had in all the other events.

She was beaming. I congratulated her.

"Thanks," said Becky. "I guess all your cheerleading didn't make a difference."

I rolled my eyes to the ceiling, sorry I had even bothered to congratulate her. But Becky didn't need to try to make me feel bad. I felt bad enough already.

I unwrapped the tape from my palms. I had managed to compete in the floor exercises, but I hadn't done very well.

"I stunk," I muttered as I pulled off my leotard.

"Don't blame yourself," said Lauren. "We all stunk."

"Yeah, you would have at least thought I could do an aerial cartwheel. I did it perfectly in practice." I waved my hands in the air. "Look judges, no hands," I said sarcastically. "But I didn't have any rhythm."

"Stop putting yourself down," said Cindi. "We lost, that's all. That one judge was against us. Let's put it behind us. Lauren said it: 'We all stunk.'"

"Cindi, you didn't stink," I said. "Even Coach Miller was impressed with you. You should have heard Patrick and Coach Miller arguing about her."

"Yeah," said Jodi, "what was that all about? I

couldn't hear, but I've never seen Patrick look so angry."

"It was nothing," muttered Cindi.

"It was, too," I said excitedly. "Patrick thought Coach Miller was trying to recruit Cindi. Patrick got mad."

"If that's true," said Becky from across the locker room, "Cindi should be flattered. Coach Miller's the best."

"How can you say that?" screamed Cindi. She sounded really upset.

"Cool down," I whispered to her.

"I hate Becky," whispered Cindi, very red in the face.

"So do I, but she actually was complimenting you."

Cindi did not cool down. In fact, she seemed more upset than ever. Cindi doesn't usually have a temper. In fact, she's the steadiest of all of us, so it was a shock to see her walk around in little circles.

"What's she so bothered about?" whispered Lauren.

Lauren is Cindi's best friend, but even she was surprised at how unhinged Cindi was by Becky's taunt. By now, we were all used to Becky's little zingers, but something in what she said seemed to have hit Cindi harder than it should have.

"I don't ever want to be an Atomic Amazon,"

said Cindi. There was something weird in her tone of voice.

"I wish Coach Miller had recruited me," said Ashley.

"Ashley, shut up," I said. I was worried about Cindi. "Coach Miller's a grade A fink. Look at the tricks he tried to play on us today."

"Well, they worked, didn't they?" said Ashley. "We lost."

"She's right," whispered Lauren, still stealing glances at Cindi. Cindi had peeled off her leotard angrily and stuffed it into her gym bag.

"Coach Miller's smart," said Becky. "There's nothing wrong with being smart."

"If you think he's so great, why aren't you an Atomic Amazon?" I snapped at Becky.

Becky just smiled at me.

"What does that smile mean?" I asked. "I think you and Coach Miller would get along great. Your personalities are alike."

"He's too much of a drill sergeant for me," said Becky. "Besides I wouldn't want to come all the way downtown."

"In other words, you're too lazy for him," muttered Cindi.

"Who put the chip on your shoulder?" asked Becky. "You're the only Pinecone who should be in *good* mood. You didn't wimp out just because of a little rip."

I looked down at my palm. It wasn't a little rip. My palms were still oozing a little bit of blood from underneath the huge blister.

"Darlene's *not* a wimp," said Cindi.

"Thank you very much," I said sarcastically. "Being not a wimp doesn't mean very much." I remember learning in history that President Nixon had gone on television and said, "I'm *not* a crook." Then it turned out he had been lying and breaking laws. Somehow Cindi saying, "Darlene's *not* a wimp" felt creepy, as if anyone except Becky would really believe that I had been a wimp.

"Well, I'm sorry," said Cindi.

"Sorry, isn't the point." Finally I had had it. I couldn't stand the way the Pinecones were acting.

"Look, Pinecones," I said. "We've got to turn ourselves around. We've got to change."

"Why should we change?" asked Jodi. "We don't want to be like the Atomic Amazons."

"We don't want to be losers, either," I said. "We've got to shape up."

"What do you have in mind?" giggled Jodi. "More shape-up exercises?"

"I don't know what I have in mind," I said, thoroughly exasperated. "It just feels like we're drifting."

"Lighten up, Darlene," said Jodi, as she slipped on her sweatshirt.

Cindi stared at me. "Give it up," she said softly.

I sighed. Well, I had tried, but turning this team around was not going to be easy.

8

Slip-Sliding Away

That night after dinner, Cindi called me. She sounded a little strange. "I just called to say hi," she said.

Cindi and I talk all the time on the phone, but this didn't sound like an I-called-to-say-hello phone call.

"Are you all right?" I asked.

"Nothing hurts," she said.

"That's not what I meant," I explained. "You sound really down."

"Losing stinks," she said.

"Don't I know it," I agreed.

Cindi sighed over the phone.

"Cin," I said, "what's with the sighs? You sound like you're in a soap opera."

"It's nothing," said Cindi. "It's just the way you sounded before . . . you sounded really angry at the Pinecones."

"I'm not," I said. "It's just that losing because we don't try makes me angry."

"I tried," said Cindi defensively.

"I know," I said. "We're trying, but we're not doing." Then I stopped myself. "I don't know why I'm talking like this."

"Yeah, well, it *has* gotten a little depressing lately," said Cindi. "I'll see you tomorrow at the gym. I'll talk to you then."

"I'm not going tomorrow," I said. "I'm visiting my great-grandmother. Remember?"

Cindi sighed again. I tried laughing at her. "Cindi, I think you're taking this sighing routine a little too far. We've lost other meets and it hasn't gotten you down."

"I feel we let Patrick down," said Cindi. "It would have been so great if we could have stuck a trophy in Coach Miller's face . . . for Patrick."

"We still have another meet in two weeks. Maybe we'll do better."

"Ha!" said Cindi. "With our team?"

"Whoa, now you're sounding like Becky."

"Sorry," said Cindi quickly. "I wouldn't talk this way with Lauren or Jodi."

I was surprised. Not only had Lauren and Cindi been best friends since kindergarten, but

I always thought of Jodi as being closer to Cindi than I was.

"It's because you're older," said Cindi. "Lauren and Jodi would go nuts if they heard me like this. Sorry to be such a first-class grouch."

"Cindi, Becky's a first-class grouch. You'll never win first prize in the grouch category. You won't even win second. Ashley has that sewn up."

Cindi started giggling and it made me feel better. "You're right," she said. "I'll see you Monday."

I hung up the phone smiling. "That's the first genuine smile I've seen on your face all night," said my mom. "Try to keep it there when you see GeeGee tomorrow."

I'm the oldest great-grandchild, and GeeGee likes me the best. I'm not bragging. That's what GeeGee says.

GeeGee's gotten very frail. That's why she can't live alone. GeeGee is a very funny old lady. And I don't mean funny-strange. She's not. She's every bit as sane as you and me. She just loves to tell people what she thinks.

Becky says mean things and pretends she's just being honest. GeeGee isn't mean. She just doesn't like it when people lie to her.

She lives in a kind of group home for old people. It's not quite a nursing home, 'cause they each have their own apartment, but the rooms are tiny, and GeeGee doesn't cook much. She eats most of her meals in the big dining room.

The food used to be lousy, but GeeGee led a protest and got the cook fired. GeeGee is quite a pistol. Sometimes I think she's not afraid of anything. Dad thinks the food at the home is still lousy, and he's always offering to take GeeGee out to eat, but GeeGee says that she likes the food, and that restaurant food is too salty.

GeeGee is tiny. I tower over her. When I was in third grade I already had a bigger shoe size than she does. GeeGee is the only one who can call me Big Foot and get away with it.

I'm not a saint, though. I don't *like* going to the home. Some of the old people there are really sad and scary. When I see them I want to dash out of there or look away. Sometimes they sit in wheelchairs and look so sad.

But I guess you can tell I *like* GeeGee and she makes going to the home worth it.

The day after the meet Dad picked me up at school and drove me to the home. I tried not to look at the people sitting in wheelchairs in front of the TV, looking as if nobody ever came to visit them.

GeeGee was in her room. She reached her hand out to me. It was bony. I took it. She looked at the rip on my palm.

"Where did you get that?" she asked.

"Gymnastics," I said.

GeeGee laughed. Sometimes she laughs at odd moments. "You take after your dad. I had to get used to seeing him all bandaged up, and now it's you. Well, I'm glad you don't think you're too pretty to get a little banged up. You wouldn't be a Broderick if you were afraid of a few bruises."

Dad gave GeeGee a peck on the cheek. "I don't think Darlene's ready for football," he said.

"Why not?" asked GeeGee. "Things are changing, Eric." Eric Broderick III is my father's real name, but he's been called "Beef" since grade school. GeeGee has always hated his nickname. "It was bad enough when it was plain 'Beef,' " she said, "but 'Big Beef' sounds like you're in a McDonald's ad." In fact, Dad has been in a McDonald's ad, but that doesn't satisfy GeeGee. She still thinks he shouldn't let himself be called "Big Beef."

"So, tell me, Darlene," she asked. "You didn't come yesterday because of your big meet. Did you at least win?"

"We got slaughtered," I said. "My hands hurt so much I couldn't grip the bar. Little Ti An couldn't stay on the beam if her life had depended on it."

GeeGee listened. She says the best way to find out about people is to shut up and let them talk.

56

I found myself telling her all about Patrick and Coach Miller's rivalry and the strange fight that they had had in front of Cindi and me.

"You didn't tell me about this," said Dad.

"I didn't feel like talking about it yesterday," I said.

"It sounds like a mess," said Dad. "Did you talk to your team? Help them sort it out?"

"Dad . . ." I sighed. "There was nothing I could do."

"Nothing?" asked GeeGee.

"Well, I cheered them on, GeeGee. In fact, some people said I was too much of a cheerleader."

"Whoever said that must be mighty stupid," said GeeGee.

I nodded my head. "Becky is," I admitted.

Dad laughed. He knows what a pain Becky can be.

"I don't care about any Becky," said GeeGee. "I want to know what you did for your team besides cheerleading. You care about them. It's up to you to inspire them."

I practically laughed out loud. *Me* inspire *them*? What did she think I was, a miracle worker? Sometimes I think that GeeGee really is getting too old.

"What are you laughing at?" asked GeeGee sharply. "Are you laughing at an old woman?"

"No, GeeGee," I said quickly.

"Darlene, you come from a long line of fighters. So don't you go thinking that you can just be a cheerleader. Brodericks aren't cheerleaders. They're leaders."

"I tried, GeeGee. I know something's wrong with the team right now, but I'm not sure exactly what."

"It's attitude," said Dad. "You're letting that Coach Miller play games with your team's mind, and maybe your coach's mind. And if you see something like that, you've got to stop it."

"Your father's right," said GeeGee.

"I can't stop it," I argued. "I'm just a kid."

GeeGee frowned at me. "It was 'just kids' who marched with Martin Luther King. And I'm just an old lady, but I don't let that stop me. If I had just sat here and listened to these old biddies whine and complain about the food, I'd still be eating nothing but mystery meat and canned vegetables. But I told them we had to organize. 'We're too old,' they cried. You can't live your life by the labels people put on you. Eric, here, he was always so big as a kid, he could have been labeled nothing but a hunk of beef. But he didn't let that label stick." GeeGee gave Dad a penetrating look. "Did you, Eric?"

"Actually, GeeGee," said my dad with a smile, "that's one label that did stick. But you're right.

Inside I didn't let anybody label me as just a piece of meat. You wouldn't let me."

"Of course not," said GeeGee. "We Brodericks don't let other people tell us who we are."

"When you hear everybody complaining, Darlene," said GeeGee, "you can't say 'I'm just a kid.' You're *not* a kid. You're thirteen."

"I know. I'm the oldest of the Pinecones, but maybe I'm too old. I don't want to be a grouch."

"Well, you're going to have to do something," said GeeGee. "Otherwise that team is just going to slip-slide away."

I didn't want the Pinecones to go slip-sliding away, but Dad and GeeGee could talk all they wanted to about me doing something about it. I *was* just a kid. Dad might be able to inspire his football team, but he was born a leader. He's always liked to take charge. And GeeGee's never had trouble telling people what to do. But I'm different, and I didn't know how I was going to inspire my team to win over a sneaky, double-dealing gymnastics coach. It was easy for Dad and GeeGee to tell me to do something. Nobody had given me any clue as to *what* I was supposed to do.

9

They Don't Sell
Inspiration at a Store

On Monday when I came into the locker room, Cindi and Lauren were giggling in a corner. I was glad to see Cindi in a much better mood.

"You seem like your old self again," I said.

Cindi grinned. "Yeah, I was just in a funk about losing."

"What happened here on Friday while I was at GeeGee's?" I asked. "Did Patrick give the old turn-the-page speech?" Whenever we lose, Patrick always tells us to "turn the page."

Cindi and Lauren exchanged guilty looks. "I wasn't here," said Cindi. "I played hooky."

"You?" I asked. I can't remember a time, except when she broke her leg, that Cindi ever missed a day of gymnastics.

"So did Lauren," said Cindi. "We just didn't feel like going. We were so far down."

If Cindi and Lauren were skipping gymnastics just because they were feeling down, we were much worse off than I had imagined.

Just then, Jodi burst into the locker room. She came right to our corner. "There you are, you finks," she said to us. She flung down her gym bag on a bench. "Where were you? I had to listen to Ashley whine all afternoon about how the four of us never treat her like a *real* Pinecone and that's why we lost. Then Ti An kept chirping in that she *never* wants to go against the Atomic Amazons again. Meanwhile, Patrick was in a foul mood. It was a great afternoon on Friday. Thanks a bunch. Somebody might have invited me to join them. Am I or am I not an original Pinecone? What did the rest of you do . . . go to the movies?"

"Slow down. Don't blame me. I was visiting GeeGee," I said. "I didn't know Cindi and Lauren weren't coming."

"We just skipped out and hung around the mall," said Cindi. "My brother dropped us off. I called Patrick from a pay phone."

"Very cute," said Jodi. "You could have at least come in and gotten me."

"We wanted to," said Cindi. "But I was afraid that if Patrick saw us we'd never have the guts to leave again."

I put on my leotard and didn't say anything, but it seemed like a weird way to think of guts. Usually I admire Cindi for her nerve, but copping out of gymnastics just because we lost a match . . . that didn't take guts, in my book. In fact, I didn't blame Jodi for feeling betrayed.

We went out into the gym. Ti An and Ashley were in the middle of the room. Ti An kept looking over at us, as if she thought we were whispering about her.

"It's good to see you back," said Patrick dryly when we all got into the gym.

Cindi blushed. I felt badly that Patrick might have thought I had played hooky, too, instead of going to visit my great-grandmother.

"We're sorry we missed Friday," said Lauren.

"I don't want to waste time with excuses," said Patrick. "There's no need to rehash Thursday's meet. We all know we have our work cut out for us. But I have an announcement to make."

"Uh-oh," whispered Jodi, a little too loud.

"Is it serious?" asked Lauren. She giggled. "The last time you told us something serious we had to face the Atomic Amazons."

"Lauren and Jodi," said Patrick, sounding annoyed. "Would you mind keeping quiet until I make my announcement?"

I squirmed a little uncomfortably. Patrick

sounded very stern, not like himself at all.

"I have to be in California for my safety recertification from the USGF. The dates for the safety course were suddenly changed, and I can't put it off for another six months. I need to have my license renewed. Unfortunately Jodi's mother is also up for her certification renewal. We had expected the course to be during our summer break, but that's impossible. Now, I've been very lucky to be able to get one of the assistant coaches at the University of Colorado to fill in for me. She also has a lot of experience as a judge. I'm sure you will learn a lot from her."

"What's her name?" I asked.

"Her name is Anna Elizabeth Kossuth."

"That's quite a mouthful," said Jodi. "Can we call her Anna?"

"She likes to be called Ms. Kossuth," said Patrick. "You can learn a lot from her. Admittedly she and I have very different styles, but it's good for you to be exposed to different coaches. Besides, she was the only one available on such short notice."

"Somehow that doesn't sound promising," I said.

"Ms. Kossuth . . . it's a tongue twister," said Lauren.

Ti An giggled.

"That's enough," said Patrick. "I expect you to show her respect and courtesy. I'll only be gone four working days."

Quickly I counted up on my fingers how long Patrick would be away. "Wait a minute!" I almost shrieked. "That's right until our meet."

"You're right, Darlene, I'll be gone until the morning of the meet. It can't be helped."

"I'll bet Coach Miller knew you were going and that's why he scheduled the meet then," said Jodi. "He's a big muckamuck in the USGF; he probably changed the dates of your course just so you'd be gone."

Patrick ran his fingers through his hair. He seemed nervous. "Jodi, I don't think even Coach Miller has enough pull to change the dates of an entire course because of one meet."

"I wouldn't put it past him," said Lauren.

"He'll do anything to beat you," said Cindi.

"Girls!" said Patrick sharply. "Don't look for excuses." He looked straight at Cindi. "I'm sorry that you think Coach Miller has some sort of a grudge against us."

"We don't *think* it," said Lauren. "He does. Why else would he try to recruit Cindi?"

"Shh!" said Cindi quickly. "I *told* you to keep it secret."

Patrick rolled his eyes. "There're no secrets in

this gym. All right, girls, I'll level with you. You all know I once worked for Coach Miller. We have different coaching styles, and sometimes it might seem as if there's a little friction between us."

"A little friction!" I said. I couldn't keep quiet any longer. "Coach Miller's the one who should be tested for safety. He is *unsafe* for the Pinecones."

Lauren, Jodi, and Cindi jumped to their feet and started clapping for me. So did Ti An. Even Ashley reluctantly got off her butt and stood up. I blushed, but I took a bow.

Patrick gave a huge sigh. "All right, Darlene, you've made your point. But we have to worry about ourselves, not about Coach Miller. Now, while I'm gone, you'll be working with Ms. Kossuth, but I want you to elect a captain to keep up your team spirit while I'm gone."

I looked immediately at Cindi. It seemed to me that Cindi had always been the natural leader of our group. Cindi comes from a big family, and even though she's the baby, she's good with groups. She doesn't get all uptight if something goes wrong. I raised my hand. "I nominate Cindi," I said.

Cindi waved her hand in the air. "I nominate Darlene," she said, and winked at me.

"Fix, fix . . ." joked Jodi, as if Cindi and I had made a deal to nominate each other. Jodi's joke made me uncomfortable.

"Are there any other nominations?" asked Patrick.

Patrick looked around the circle. Ti An picked at her leotard. Ashley was sitting with her legs crossed, looking up at Patrick with perfect attention.

Lauren and Jodi exchanged glances. I wondered if both of them wanted to be captain and were hurt that they hadn't been nominated.

"All right," said Patrick. He tore a piece of paper from his clipboard and ripped it into six pieces. He handed out the paper and six pencils. "Let's do this quickly. Scatter around the gym and think about your choice for a couple of minutes. Don't talk to each other. Then bring me back your slips."

"What'll we do if it's a tie?" asked Lauren. "There're six of us."

"Then I'll cast the deciding vote," said Patrick.

I caught Cindi's eye as I scuttled over to the bench. Becky walked by. "What's this?" she asked. "Has Patrick sent the Pinecones back to kindergarten for some remedial writing?"

"We're voting for captain," I said. "We need privacy."

"Well, excuse me," said Becky. She went and joined her own teammates.

I thought for a moment about voting for myself. When I first found out that politicians voted for themselves, I was surprised. Mom told me that you can't run for office unless you think you'll be the best person for the job.

If I *were* captain, maybe I'd be able to do something about the way the team was acting. I knew it would make GeeGee and Mom and Dad proud, but I wasn't sure it was the best thing for the team. I thought being captain would be a good thing for Cindi.

I started to write down Cindi's name but, boy, was it hard. I blinked. I actually *wanted* to write my own name down there.

Quickly I just scribbled Cindi's name and folded the paper.

I handed it to Patrick just as Ashley was handing in her vote. Patrick gathered the other slips. He turned his back to us and spread out the slips of paper on the balance beam.

Then he crumpled them up and put them in his pocket.

"Darlene," said Patrick, "I think you'll make a very good captain." He shook my hand.

I tried to keep from grinning too hard. I couldn't believe how good it felt to have won.

"Congratulations," said Cindi. She gave me a hug. There's nothing petty about Cindi. I hugged her back.

"What was the vote?" asked Ashley.

"It doesn't matter," said Cindi, but I caught her stealing a glance at Patrick. I wondered myself what the vote had been. Had I only gotten in because Patrick had been forced to chose between us?

"Darlene is our captain. Now let's get to work," said Patrick.

We worked on our floor routine, and I had so much adrenalin I did my aerial cartwheel without needing Patrick to spot me once. I tried to act cool all during practice, but I was flying. Me! Captain! Maybe my cheerleading had made a difference. I was the oldest; maybe the other Pinecones looked up to me. Now I could really do something to turn things around.

"We should make you Captain every day," Patrick whispered to me as he patted me on the back.

I grinned at him. "What's a captain supposed to do? Am I super-cheerleader or what?"

"No," said Patrick. "A leader who cheers the others on, inspires them. It's different."

"Inspires, that's GeeGee's word," I mumbled. But Patrick wasn't listening. He was busy spotting Lauren on her floor routine. Patrick's job as coach was clear. He always knew what he was supposed to do. But I was going to need plenty of inspiration if I was going to make a good captain. Unfortunately, although I love to shop, I don't know of any stores that sell inspiration.

10

Pathetic is Becky's Favorite Word

"Ms. Kossuth! Watch me!" lisped Ashley. Ms. Kossuth looked up from the beam where I was trying to get through my routine. I had fallen about six times and I needed just a little help trying to do my handstand into a forward roll. If Ms. Kossuth would just put a hand up to steady me, I would have been all right.

Instead she asked me to hop down from the beam and look at a diagram she drew on her clipboard. I don't learn well from diagrams. I learn by doing. But Ms. Kossuth believed in doing things her way and that meant endless diagramming and *no* spotting. She said that she didn't believe in spotting. "The gymnast who is spotted a lot thinks she's successful, but she's not. You will not have a spot in competition." Personally I think she didn't like spotting because she was worried her stomach would get in the way.

Ms. Kossuth had gray hair, and she was stout. She didn't look like a gymnastics coach. First of all, she wasn't young. I mean, Jodi's mom isn't real young, but at least she looks like an athlete.

It wasn't as if Ms. Kossuth didn't know gymnastics; she did. But she sure didn't have Patrick's sense of humor. She didn't like us joking around *at all* while we were working.

Patrick never lets us get away with fooling around too much, but he doesn't mind when we crack jokes while we're waiting in line, and we have gotten used to doing it. It keeps us loose.

Now we were wound tight. Instead of cracking jokes, we were about to crack each other's heads.

I figured we were going to be slaughtered by the Atomic Amazons the following week. They wouldn't even need bows and arrows. They could just blow on us and we'd crumble.

"Darlene, you must concentrate. You are not concentrating," said Ms. Kossuth. "You must think of the beam as just a narrow piece of floor."

I tried to think of the beam as a narrow piece of floor, but it just kept getting narrower. And usually I like beam! I couldn't wait to get off.

Finally I had fallen off enough times. Ms. Kossuth let me do my roundoff dismount. I landed crooked and came down hard, almost twisting my ankle.

"Your right hand was at a sixty-degree angle, and it should have been at a ninety-degree angle. That's why you fell," said Ms. Kossuth.

I grunted. As if I needed a geometry lesson to figure out why I had fallen! I didn't understand what she was talking about. I went to stand at the back of the line.

"Ms. Kossuth!" said Ashley, even though it was Ti An's turn on the beam. "I finally understand where my head is supposed to be when I start my dismount."

"I'd like to put her head in the sand," muttered Jodi. "That's where it belongs."

"Ashley's or Ms. Kossuth's?" I asked.

"Both," said Jodi.

"I think Ms. Kossuth is another of Coach Miller's plots against us," whispered Cindi.

Ms. Kossuth glanced over at us. "Girls! Stop that giggling and talking. You all have work to do."

It was only our second day with Ms. Kossuth, and already we were sick of her . . . everybody except Ashley, who pretended to adore Ms. Kossuth. Ashley is bad enough with Patrick, constantly wanting his attention, but she was even worse with Ms. Kossuth. I think Ashley suffers from permanent teacher's-pet-itis.

" 'Ms. Kossuth, watch me,' " Jodi sneered at Ashley. "Can't you think of anything else to say?"

"I did it almost perfectly," said Ashley. "I wanted Ms. Kossuth to see me."

"She's been *seeing* you. Pity the rest of us that have to *hear* your squeaky little voice."

"Hey, Jodi, chill out," I said, but Cindi took Jodi's side. "Ashley, you've been a pain in the neck ever since Patrick's been gone."

"Ashley was a pain in the neck even before Patrick left," said Jodi. "Now she's a pain in the — "

"Jodi!" I snapped. Ashley looked like she was near tears.

"What?" demanded Jodi.

"You can't talk to Ashley like that. She's still a Pinecone."

"Since when have *you* become her big defender?" demanded Jodi.

"Since she became Captain," muttered Cindi.

My mouth dropped open, but before I could answer Cindi, she was upside down, doing a perfect back walkover. As she arched over into a handstand, her toes were pointed, her back so limber that she looked like she was liquid, flowing from her toes to her hands and back again.

"Jodi!" shouted Ms. Kossuth. "You're next."

Jodi gave me a dirty look. Ashley put her hands

on her hips. "Honestly I think Jodi's being impossible," she said. "I don't think she's adjusting at all well to Ms. Kossuth. I think Ms. Kossuth has a lot to teach us, but this team just won't learn. We're going to be a mess when we meet the Atomic Amazons. We're falling apart."

"Ashley, button up," I said.

"Everybody always tells me to shut up," whined Ashley. "But you never pick on the other Pinecones. It's not fair."

"Ashley, can't you think of something else to say for a change?" I pleaded. "I'm sick of hearing 'it's not fair.' "

I watched Jodi up on the beam. She was rushing through her routine. She looked sloppy. She fell off trying to do a forward roll.

"Jodi, your hips weren't aligned with the beam. They have to be in a straight line," said Ms. Kossuth. "Square your shoulders with the beam before you start the roll."

"I was doing an off-the-beam roll," joked Jodi. "It's a new move. You'll see it in the '92 Olympics."

"I don't think so," said Ms. Kossuth seriously.

Jodi bit her lip. Ms. Kossuth patted the beam for Jodi to remount.

"I hurt myself," said Jodi, rubbing her hip.

"Come on, Jodi," said Ms. Kossuth calmly. "Get back up here."

"I hurt myself," said Jodi, rubbing her hip even more exaggeratedly.

"She's dogging it," whispered Ashley.

Cindi grabbed Ashley by the elbow. "I'd like to dog you," she said.

"Ms. Kossuth!" Ashley cried out. "Cindi's hurting me."

Cindi tried to clap her hand over Ashley's mouth. Ms. Kossuth looked up.

"Cindi!" she said sharply. "Take your hands off Ashley. Girls, I am ashamed of you. Jodi, go put an ice pack on your hip. As for the rest of you, instead of pushing each other around, I want you to do push-ups. I want you to do twenty handstand push-ups. Divide up into pairs and spot each other."

"Cindi, that was stupid," I whispered angrily to Cindi. "For goodness' sake, Ashley's just a kid."

"She bugs me," muttered Cindi.

Handstand push-ups are about the hardest conditioning we do. You have to do a handstand against the wall and then slowly bend your arms and push back up. If you don't have enough strength, you fall right on your head. One partner holds your feet and tries to steady you, but you still have to do all the work by yourself, and your arms ache, believe me.

Cindi was my partner. She's really strong. She

did her twenty without shaking, but when she stood up she rubbed her biceps.

I kicked up into a handstand. I bent my elbows and tried to straighten them. Cindi had just a light touch on my ankles. She wasn't really helping at all. I'm not as strong as she is, and I needed her to pull on my ankles to keep me steady.

I grunted, hoping she'd get the hint that I needed more help. But Cindi didn't do anything for me.

Finally after about six push-ups, my arms were like spaghetti. I bent them and no matter how hard I tried, I couldn't straighten them.

"Cindi!" I whispered upside down, through gritted teeth. "Pull!"

"What's the matter, Captain?" asked Cindi. "Running out of fuel?"

Finally I collapsed.

I rolled over on the mats and looked up at Cindi. At least she looked ashamed. "Sorry," she muttered.

"What's wrong with you, Cindi?"

"It's not me," said Cindi. "It's the whole team. We're falling apart."

"That's what Ashley said."

Cindi looked surprised. "Ashley?!"

"Ashley," I repeated.

Ms. Kossuth called us together. "All right, girls, you've done enough for today. I'll see you on Monday, and we'll do our final preparations for your meet."

" 'Final preparations,' " muttered Jodi. "She means preparing our coffins for the Amazons to bury us."

"That does it," I said. I raised my hand. "Ms. Kossuth, may I make an announcement? I'm holding a team meeting this weekend on Saturday at four."

"What for?" asked Cindi.

"Because as captain, I've got to find some way of pulling this team together."

"What if I don't want to come?" asked Ashley.

"You have to," I said. "You're a Pinecone. I want every Pinecone at that meeting."

"I think that's a good idea, Darlene," said Ms. Kossuth.

I wished she had kept her mouth shut. Her liking it was a kiss of death.

We had been falling apart even before Patrick had had to go away. Now we were a walking disaster area. And I was captain. Maybe the other kids couldn't see it the way I did. We acted like we were the same old Pinecones, but we weren't. We weren't being funny anymore. We were being pathetic. And I *hated* that. Pathetic was Becky's favorite word for us.

11

No Easy Answers

I was really nervous. I paced around my living room. Deirdre tried to follow me, but I was going too fast for her. Deirdre knows she can move much faster when she crawls. After all, she's only been walking a few months, and she's a real speed demon on all fours.

She dropped down to a crawl and continued to follow me. I got down on the floor with her and picked her up. "Okay, smart one," I said. "What are you going to say to the team?" It was three-thirty on Saturday and I still had no real idea of what a team meeting was going to accomplish.

Sometimes I love to talk to Deirdre. She smiles at you, and you don't have to make sense.

I sighed and lay down on the floor, bouncing Deirdre on my stomach. "Can't you think of anything inspiring?" I asked her. She burped. I cracked up.

"What's so funny?" asked Dad, coming into the room. He dropped down on the floor beside us.

"I asked Deirdre what I should say to the team, and she burped," I said. I handed Deirdre to Dad.

"Are the Pinecones having problems with Ms. Kossuth?" he asked.

"It's not really her," I said. "I mean, she's strict, and I don't love her, but all the Pinecones are sniping at each other. I think we're just scared 'cause Patrick's away. But I can't think of anything I can say that will make a difference."

"I think it's a good idea that you called this team meeting," said Dad, "away from the coaches, away from the other gymnasts."

"That's what I thought, too, but I don't know what I'm supposed to say." I looked up at my father. "If you say, 'say what's in your heart,' I'll throw this pillow at you." Dad always tells me to say what's in my heart. It drives me nuts.

"Say what's in your heart," said Dad.

I threw the pillow at him. "Come on, Dad. You've had lots of team meetings. What good do they do?"

"Sometimes they don't do any good. Sometimes if we're in a slump, nothing helps except finally getting out of the slump."

"Thanks. That's very encouraging."

"But sometimes a meeting helps clear the air," said Dad.

The doorbell rang. "That must be them," I said. Dad stood up with Deirdre in his arms. I had asked him to stay out of sight and to keep Deirdre and Debi busy. I didn't want any distractions when I talked to the Pinecones.

"Say what's in your heart," he whispered to me. "Come on, Deirdre, let's get out of here."

"Thanks, Dad," I said. I licked my lips. I wanted to change things, but I didn't know how.

I went to the door. Jodi, Cindi, and Lauren all had arrived together on their bikes. Jodi was staying at Cindi's house while her mother was away.

They looked as nervous as I did. Jodi took off her jacket and threw it on a chair in the hall. She started downstairs to the playroom where we almost always meet.

But I didn't want everybody to go down there. Downstairs we always fooled around with the Ping-Pong table, the low beam, Dad's exercise bicycle, and treadmill. Downstairs there were too many distractions.

I led the gang into the living room. It's not formal. It's got two huge comfortable sofas and a couple of leather chairs. The biggest thing in the room is a huge granite coffee table, solid enough so that even Dad can put his feet up on it and not tip it over. The living room is two stories high, and the windows look out on a stand of aspen trees in our backyard. It's not as if Mom and Dad tell me not to use it for my friends — it's just not where we usually sit.

"Aren't we going downstairs?" Jodi asked.

"No," I said.

The doorbell rang again. I jumped up to let in Ti An and Ashley, who were in the middle of an argument. "We're late because Ashley wasn't ready," said Ti An before she had even taken off her jacket.

"We're late because Ti An's mom didn't know where your house was," said Ashley. "I wasn't late. Where's your dad?"

"He's downstairs, and we're up here," I said. "And I don't care why you're late."

I led Ti An into the living room. Jodi was playing on Deirdre's rocking dragon that we keep in the living room. It's a rocking horse in the shape of a dragon. Dad found it at a crafts fair, and he likes to rock on it himself. Luckily, it's built close to the ground so he doesn't break it.

"Okay," I said, coughing a little nervously. "I'm calling this meeting together. Jodi, get off the rocking dragon. We've got to really talk."

Jodi looked a little taken aback. "Well, okay, but I was thinking that the rocking dragon reminds me of Ms. Kossuth."

Lauren giggled nervously.

"Ms. Kossuth isn't the real problem," I said.

"She's built like a dragon," said Jodi.

"That's not funny," I said. "And it's not helpful."

"What is your problem?" asked Cindi.

"It's not *my* problem. It's *our* problem," I said. "We're not acting like a team anymore. I think something happened to us after that meet with the Atomic Amazons. We let Coach Miller get to us."

"He didn't get to *me*!" protested Cindi. "You all think I was tempted because he was nice to me, but I wasn't!"

"I don't think you were tempted, but it *did* get to you. You've been jumpy as a cat ever since that meet. Anybody would have been flattered. You're only human," I said.

"Maybe Cindi does want to be an Atomic Amazon," said Ashley.

"Shut up, twerp!" yelled Cindi. "You're the sorriest excuse for a Pinecone that I've ever seen."

"You never treat me like I'm part of the team anyway," whined Ashley.

Ti An looked embarrassed by all the emotion.

Her feet were curled up underneath her on the couch. Lauren tried to pretend nothing was going on. She looked out the window at the aspen trees as if she were counting branches for a science project.

"Ashley, we would treat you as a member of the team if you didn't try to act like a miniature Becky all the time," I said. "If you've got to imitate Becky, do it as a gymnast, not as a person."

"Right on, Darlene!" said Cindi.

"And, Cindi, stop goading Ashley. You react to every little thing Ashley says. Ashley *is* a Pinecone. She's a part of this team. It's not just the four of us anymore."

"Where do you get off telling us what to do?" demanded Cindi.

"You voted for me as captain."

Cindi just glared at me. "I nominated you, but don't be so sure I voted for you," she snapped.

Lauren stopped looking out the window and stared at Cindi.

I felt my face get hot. "That's not the point. The point is that I *am* captain, and we have to pull together. That means that you can't keep picking on Ashley every time you get in a rotten mood. It's bad for the team."

"Oh yeah, since when are you Ashley's great friend?"

"Cindi!" I snapped. "For the good of the team, just shut up."

Everybody froze. I had never spoken to Cindi like that.

Ashley giggled. She couldn't have picked a worse moment. "Finally," she said, "someone else is being told to shut up."

Cindi glared at me. "Are you putting me in the same category as Ashley?" she demanded.

"Ashley *is* a Pinecone," I said. "That's the problem. None of us are acting like Pinecones anymore."

"You can't tell me to shut up," said Cindi. "We voted you in as captain. We didn't vote you in as bully."

"Cindi," warned Lauren. "Come on. . . ."

But Cindi ignored her. She got up out of the chair and stormed out of the living room. I ran after her. "Where are you going?" I demanded.

"Out!" said Cindi.

"You can't leave. It's a team meeting."

"Just watch me!" said Cindi. I ran after her, but she was already on her bike and pedaling furiously down the driveway.

The rest of the Pinecones ran to the door. There was an embarrassed silence. "Boy, and I thought I was the one with the temper," said Jodi finally.

"Don't worry, Darlene," said Lauren. "Cindi'll be okay."

"Is the meeting over?" asked Ti An in a tiny voice.

I sighed. "I guess so," I said. One by one the Pinecones left.

Dad came back upstairs. He looked around the living room. "Quick meeting?" he said.

"It was a disaster," I wailed.

"What happened?" Dad asked.

I explained to Dad what had happened. I hiccupped. I was trying hard not to cry.

"You've got to wait it out, honey. Leading a team isn't like in the movies. You just don't make one inspirational speech and everything changes. It's hard to turn a team around."

"But what if I made things worse? Cindi's mad at me. Cindi's never been mad at me before. Nobody's been mad at me like that before."

"She'll get over it. She's your friend. What did you get mad at her for?"

"She always lets Ashley get to her. She's so busy thinking up clever retorts to Ashley that she's not thinking straight. I told her to quit worrying about Ashley. I think Cindi got really frazzled by Coach Miller, but she won't admit it."

"I've been on teams where we've been so busy fighting each other, we left all the adrenalin in the locker room."

"But Cindi's always been my friend. I like Cindi. Ashley's a dope."

"Captains have to be a little bit like coaches," said Dad. "You can't play favorites."

"Couldn't you just say something comforting like 'Everything's going to be okay'?" I complained.

Dad gave me a hug. "I would, but GeeGee taught me never to give kids easy answers."

12

A Great Idea
. . . Maybe

I called Lauren on Sunday to find out if Cindi was still mad at me. "She's not talking," said Lauren.

"Even to you?" I exclaimed.

"Well, she's talking to me, though she won't talk about gymnastics or what happened at the meeting, but don't worry."

"How can you say 'don't worry'?" I exclaimed. "Cindi walked out on me! Do you think I should call her?" I asked.

I could almost see Lauren shrugging over the phone. "I'd leave it alone," she said.

But I couldn't. I'm a worrier. People don't think I am because I look calm, and I'm big. People never think that big people are worriers, but I worry all the time.

I couldn't just let it alone. The idea of waiting was killing me.

I picked up the phone and called Cindi. Her brother Jared answered the phone. "Darlene!" he said cheerfully. I wasn't in the mood to chat. "Can I talk to Cindi?" I asked.

I didn't realize it, but I was holding my breath while I heard Jared calling Cindi. What if she refused to come to the phone?

But she didn't.

"Cindi," I said.

"Wait," said Cindi. "Before you say anything, I've got something to say." I couldn't breathe. "I've got something to say" struck me as the scariest words in the English language.

"I'm sorry," Cindi muttered over the phone.

I was so relieved that I practically threw the receiver in the air for joy. "Cindi, I'm sorry, too. I didn't mean to upset you. . . ."

"No, it's my fault," said Cindi.

"No, it was my fault," I said.

"My fault," said Cindi. Soon we were giggling. Finally I heard Cindi's brother calling her in the background.

"I've got to go," said Cindi quickly. "I just wanted to say, 'I'm sorry.' "

"Me, too," I said.

I hung up the phone. I raised my hands over my head and did a little dance.

"You look like one of our rookies in the end zone," said Dad. "Don't you know that touchdown dances are against the rules these days?" Dad was grinning at me. "What's the good news?"

"Cindi apologized," I said. "I feel so good."

"What did you say?" asked Dad.

"I said I was sorry, too."

"What did you have to be sorry for?" Dad asked me.

I stared at him. "I was the one who got her upset," I said. "Besides, when you and Mom fight you both say you're sorry. Cindi and I just had a stupid little fight, and it's over. Don't mess with me."

"But nothing's solved," said Dad.

"Cindi and I are friends again," I argued.

"Friendship wasn't the issue. You and Cindi aren't so fragile that your friendship would fall apart. You've got more respect for Cindi than that, and I'll bet she has more respect for you. But you're the captain, and you're the oldest, and you're letting Cindi get away with murder. She doesn't have to apologize to you. She's got to stop picking on Ashley or you'll never be a team."

"I can't make people stop picking on Ashley. She's a pain in the neck."

"Is she a good gymnast?" Dad asked.

"Yes," I admitted.

"Well, learning to be part of a team means having to tolerate all kinds of pains in the butt."

"Thank you very much for that leadership advice," I said sarcastically.

Dad threw up his hands.

"What does that mean?" I asked suspiciously.

"Nothing," said Dad. "You don't want my advice any more than Cindi wanted yours."

I narrowed my eyes at him. I hate it when Dad gets off one of those zingers that are true.

"Okay," I said, giving up. "What's your advice?"

"You're captain of the team, not just Cindi's friend, and if she's in a snit about something, you can't be grateful just because Cindi said she was sorry to you. You've got to think of the whole team."

"But Cindi's way more important to me than Ashley," I wailed. "Cindi's my friend."

"And Ashley's your teammate," said Dad.

I growled at him. "Maybe I should resign as captain."

"Maybe you should think of a way to bring your team together," said Dad. "Different things work for different teams. Think of all the weird things I've tried."

I started to laugh. "Yeah, remember the year your team had the swami in to teach you meditation?" I put my index fingers and thumbs together to form two perfect circles. "Ommm-mmm," I hummed.

"It worked a little," said Dad. "We used to sit in the locker room with all our padding on going 'Ommmmmm.' But at least it was something we all did together as a team."

"Yeah, great," I muttered. "I'll get them all to meditate. I can just see Ashley giggling and Cindi punching her."

"You have to do something to bring this team together before your next meet," said Dad. "When are Jodi's mom and Patrick coming back?"

"They won't be flying in until the morning of the meet," I said.

"Well, you'd better do something," said Dad. "Cindi saying 'I'm sorry' isn't going to score any points with the judges. You used to think the Pinecones were special. You'd better find a way to bring back that feeling or you'll never succeed as captain."

"Thanks for bringing me down, Dad," I muttered.

Dad was right. The Pinecones had been special. I remembered Jodi saying we had the best sense of humor of any team in Denver. That was what made us special. We worked hard, but we laughed a lot. We were funny. But lately we hadn't been laughing.

That's when I got my great idea. Well, maybe it wasn't great, but at least it was an idea.

13

The United Pinecones

On Monday, Cindi ignored Ashley in the locker room. Ashley sidled up to me. "Is Cindi still on our team?" she asked.

"Of course," I said. "It takes more than one fight to kill the Pinecones."

"But she walked out of a team meeting," said Ashley. "If I walked out of a team meeting, you'd all be meeting again just to kick me out."

"She's got a point," muttered Jodi. "Let's kick Ashley out."

"Jodi, don't," I warned. "And Ashley. You're a Pinecone and life's not fair."

"Well, it should be," pouted Ashley. But then she giggled.

I laughed.

"What are you laughing at?" asked Cindi.

"Ashley's right," I said. "Life should be fair."

Ashley giggled again. Even Cindi smiled.

"Let's get out to gymnastics. Ms. Kossuth is waiting for us," I said dryly.

Ms. Kossuth was sitting in the middle of the floor mats with what looked like a thousand diagrams around her. "Girls," said Ms. Kossuth, "I want to polish your floor routines."

"Wax or no wax?" asked Jodi.

Ms. Kossuth looked up at Jodi.

"Excuse me?" she said.

"What kind of polish are we going to use on our floor routines?" Jodi asked.

"Maybe we can use the wax in Ashley's ears," said Cindi.

Lauren started giggling. I didn't laugh.

I raised my hand. "Ms. Kossuth, as captain, may I say something to the team in private?"

Ms. Kossuth gave me an appraising look. She looked at her watch. "I will give you two minutes," she said. Ms. Kossuth gathered up her papers.

"What's this all about?" Cindi asked. "We just had a team meeting. It was a disaster."

"Cindi, apologize to Ashley for that crack about her earwax. It wasn't funny."

"Whoa," said Cindi. She was still kind of laughing. "I apologized to you, but I don't have to apologize to Ashley."

"Yes, you do," I said. "You're being selfish, and you're hurting the team. Every time we crack a joke *at* each other instead of *with* each other, we're hurting the team. I've thought a lot about what's been happening to us. The Pinecones are special just because we can joke around. We're special because we're funny. But it doesn't help us when we start making jokes *about* each other. We've got to go back to making jokes about the Atomic Amazons, not each other. You're all acting as if we've already lost tomorrow's match. Well, I'm here to tell you we haven't."

Cindi bit her lip. "I'm sorry, Ashley," she muttered finally.

"Well, you should be," said Ashley, prissily. "You always make fun of me."

"Ashley," I said, "cut it out, too. You'd rather pick fights than fight the Amazons. Let's concentrate on tomorrow."

"Yeah, think about all the dirty tricks Coach Miller will pull on us," said Lauren.

I grinned. Lauren looked at me suspiciously. "What are you grinning about?" she asked.

"Well, remember I said what was special about the Pinecones was our sense of humor?"

Lauren nodded. "I agree with you."

"Who doesn't have a sense of humor?" I asked.

"Ms. Kossuth," said Cindi.

"Besides her," I said.

"Coach Darrell Miller," said Ti An excitedly.

"Bingo," I said. "He's tried to play a lot of dirty tricks on us, but I think if we played a *funny* trick on him, he'd go up the wall."

"What do you have in mind?" Cindi asked.

I gathered my team into a huddle and told them my secret plan.

Cindi laughed out loud. She slapped me on the back. "Captain, you are too much," she said.

"How about the rest of you?" I asked. "Let's take a vote."

I asked everybody to raise her hand if she liked my plan.

One by one, each one raised her hand. Even Ashley. The Pinecones were united.

We went back to Ms. Kossuth. I took a deep breath. Now was the hardest part. I would have to sell my plan to her. But to my surprise, Ms. Kossuth turned out to have a sense of humor after all. She got a sly smile on her face when I told her about my plan.

"I see nothing in the rule book against it," she said. For a second I'd have to say she had an almost wicked smile on her face. Then it disappeared.

"Girls," she said primly, "it's time to practice

your floor exercise." The music for our floor exercise is a rinky-dink piano playing "As Time Goes By." It's pathetic, but I watched the Pinecones go through their paces, and I knew *we* weren't pathetic. We were Pinecones again.

14

Remember, We're a Team

Mom drove me to the gym after school on the day of the meet. "At least you have the home court advantage," she said. "When's Patrick supposed to be back?"

"He was supposed to be back this morning. I hope he doesn't mind what we're doing. Maybe I should have tried to check it out with him."

"If I know Patrick, he'll love it. Go in there and get ready. Dad'll be here soon with your secret weapon."

I jumped out of the car and practically skipped into the gym. Jodi and Cindi were already in the locker room. "There you are!" exclaimed Jodi. "Finally!"

I looked at my watch. It was still early. I looked around the locker room. "What do you mean 'finally'? I'm here early."

"We've got a disaster on our hands," cried Jodi.

"Is somebody hurt?" I asked quickly.

Jodi shook her head.

"Sick?" I asked.

"No," wailed Jodi, "it's worse than that. Patrick's not here. We're going to have Battleship Kossuth as our coach for the meet. My mom called from the airport in California. They're fogged in. They don't know when they're going to get here. Patrick wishes us luck. He sent us a message to do the best we can."

"Great," said Cindi. She sat down on one of the benches and pulled on her gymnastics slippers.

Just then Ti An and Ashley came into the locker room. "I can't wait to see Patrick," said Ti An. "I missed him so much."

"I can't believe it!" stormed Cindi. "The fates are against us."

"What fates?" Ti An asked. "Is something wrong with Patrick?"

"His plane is just late," I said. "Cindi, calm down. It's not the end of the world."

"We'll be a laughingstock out there," said Cindi. "Ms. Kossuth will try to give us complicated explanations and she'll start showing us diagrams. The Atomic Amazons will be cleaning up — "

I clapped my hand over Cindi's mouth.

"You always get nervous before a meet," I said.

Cindi took a deep breath. "Yeah, you're right, but this time I have a right to be nervous."

I shook my head. "No, you don't," I said. "You've forgotten the Pinecones' secret weapon."

Cindi rolled her eyes toward the ceiling. "You don't really think that little trick is going to make a difference," she said.

Ti An had a worried look on her face.

"Absolutely," I said with more confidence than I felt. "It's going to make all the difference in the world. Come on, team. Let's go meet our real fate."

"Did you say feet or fate?" asked Lauren.

"No jokes," I said. "We've got to act like this is completely serious, or we'll never pull it off."

Lauren stared at me. "You're serious, aren't you?"

"You'd better believe it," I said.

We walked out onto the gym floor. The Atomic Amazons were already warming up. Ms. Kossuth was sitting on a bench in the corner, sorting out her diagrams.

"There's Barking Barney," said Jodi, giving a shy wave to a pudgy man who was already sitting in the front row. "He said he was going to come see me."

"Where are his dogs?" Ashley asked.

Jodi put her hands on her hips. "He wouldn't bring them to a meet. Don't be stupid."

"Jodi, don't start in on Ashley. Remember, we're a team."

"Shhh," said Cindi, looking at the door. "I think our secret weapon is arriving."

15

Grandiose Gladys

Coach Miller stared at the gnarled old lady with skin the color of rich black coffee, who was dressed in a blue sequined turban, and wearing a purple feather boa around her neck. Dad was behind her, pushing the wheelchair. He looked even bigger than usual next to such a tiny lady. It had been GeeGee's idea to use the wheelchair. I thought it might be going too far, but GeeGee was really into it. She talked the home into letting her borrow it.

She wheeled right onto the gym floor. The Atomic Amazons all stopped to stare at her. "Excuse me," said Coach Miller. "There are seats for the handicapped over there." He pointed to a space next to the bleachers.

"I am not handicapped," said GeeGee sweeping the boa around her neck and hitting Coach Miller. "You are the one with the handicapped brain."

Coach Miller looked around for help. "Where's Patrick?" he asked, sounding very annoyed.

"His plane has been delayed. I'm here in his place," said GeeGee.

"Wait a minute," said Coach Miller. "I happen to know that Anna Elizabeth Kossuth coached the Pinecones in Patrick's absence and she's already here."

"Bet you can't say Anna Elizabeth Kossuth three times fast," said GeeGee.

Ms. Kossuth got up off the bench. She came over and bent down and shook GeeGee's hand. "I'm so glad that you could come," she said.

"You know this woman?" asked Coach Miller.

"By reputation," said Ms. Kossuth. "I'm honored to have her expertise." And I thought Ms. Kossuth didn't have a sense of humor.

"What expertise?" sputtered Coach Miller. "Whoever you are, I'm afraid you will have to sit over there with the parents and other friends of the gymnasts."

"My name is Grandiose Gladys. I am the Pinecones' Inner-Outer Winner Coach."

"She is," I said quickly.

Coach Miller crossed his arms over his chest.

" 'Inner-Outer Winner,' " he repeated mockingly. The Atomic Amazons gathered around him. They all crossed their arms over their chests, too. Monkey see, monkey do.

"I open the inner door so each Pinecone can let her winner out the outer door into the winner's circle," said GeeGee, as if she were making perfect sense.

Coach Miller giggled. He had a surprisingly high-pitched giggle. Dad crossed his huge arms across his chest, mimicking Coach Miller, but he dwarfed him.

"Grandiose Gladys works for the Denver Broncos," said Dad. He leaned in toward Coach Miller. "She's our secret weapon."

Dad said it loudly enough so that all the Atomic Amazons could hear.

Then he wheeled GeeGee to the side. GeeGee swept her boa out of the way of the wheels. "Pinecones roll over," she said. "The same way you will roll over the Amazons to victory."

The Atomic Amazons all started whispering among themselves and pointing to GeeGee.

GeeGee ignored them. She pointed to the floor.

Cindi went first, then Lauren, then Jodi, Ti An, and Ashley. They did a series of somersaults away from the Atomic Amazons. Amazingly, they were great somersaults. They were tight and controlled, but fast.

"Is that fair that they have an inspirational coach?" squeaked one of the Atomic Amazons.

"How come we don't?" asked another Amazon.

"Don't worry about it, girls," growled Coach Miller.

"But that lady works for the Denver Broncos. Isn't that against the amateur rules?" said one of the Amazons.

Coach Miller thumbed through the green book of points. But I had already looked through it. "There's nothing in it that says a team can't have their own inner-outer winner coach," I said.

"Who are you?" asked Coach Miller.

"I'm the captain of the team," I said. Then I put my hands over my head and did a perfect dive somersault onto the mats to join my teammates gathered around the winningest guru in all of sports — Grandiose Gladys.

"All right, girls," said GeeGee. "Sit cross-legged in front of me in a very straight line. Close your eyes."

We all did as we were told.

Very slowly, GeeGee directed Dad to wheel her up to each Pinecone. She brushed her feather boa over each of our heads.

I peaked from underneath my eyelashes. I could see the Atomic Amazons all staring at us, wondering what secret powers we were getting from Grandiose Gladys' boa. Let them wonder.

I felt the feather boa brush over me.

"May your inner door open to the wonder of winning," said GeeGee.

"What does the feather mean?" whispered Ti An.

"Just don't giggle," I warned her.

Finally GeeGee instructed us to open our eyes.

"Now I'm going to be serious," she said. "Girls, I want you to go out there and fight like tigers to win."

"GeeGee," I said. "that doesn't sound like the Guru of the Inner Door."

"Forget that garbage," said GeeGee. "Go out there and win."

"Now you're talking," I said. "Come on, team. Let's do it!"

16

We're the Pinecones and We're Hot

The Atomic Amazons went first on the vault. Normally that's one of their best events.

Cindi grabbed my hand as our opponent saluted the judge. "I hope we psyched them out," she whispered.

"Wait," I whispered back.

The Atomic Amazon got over the horse all right, but she sank to her knees and then fell face forward on her landing. She looked like she wanted to cry when she stood up.

"Too bad. They can't open the inner door," Jodi said loudly.

"Shh," I warned Jodi. It was one thing to try to psych out the Atomic Amazons before the meet, but now that we were actually into competition, it was time to get serious. I didn't want to give Coach Miller any excuses to call us for unsportswomanlike behavior.

I think our little act with GeeGee worked. The Atomic Amazons lost their confidence. They got so worried about the winning "secrets" Grandiose Gladys had given us that they couldn't concentrate. They messed up all over the place.

Finally it was our turn.

I was the first one up on the vault. The first one up is supposed to set the table for the team, giving the judges a high standard. I was the captain. I was the leader. I couldn't let my team down now; too much depended on it.

I raised my hand to salute the judge. I was doing a handstand vault. It's the hardest vault that I can do, but I felt I was ready.

I took off down the runway. I hit the springboard just right, but when I went up in the air I must have twisted my shoulder because my hand slipped on the vault, and I almost crashed headfirst into the leather.

I could hear Ms. Kossuth gasp because it must have looked like I was going to hurt myself.

I slipped down the backside of the vault and landed hard on my butt. I saved myself, but I ruined my vault.

I could feel my face get hot as I stood up.

I saluted the judge again and bit my lip. Maybe I could make up for it on the second vault.

Cindi came and patted me on the back. "You'll do it this time," she said.

I nodded.

"Do it for Grandiose Gladys!" yelled Lauren from the sidelines.

I saluted the judge a second time. This time I misjudged my step onto the springboard. I went up at a funny angle, and I knew I'd never make a handstand. I tucked my feet underneath me to do a tuck vault. It's a much lower-scoring vault, and besides, I didn't do it very well. All the judges knew I was supposed to be doing a handstand vault.

I couldn't believe that just when we really had a chance to pull off a win, I had fouled up.

The judges were huddled together to decide my score. Ashley was next up for the Pinecones.

"Thanks for setting the table for us, Captain," she said sarcastically. "You set the table for garbage."

I grabbed Ashley by the elbow and pushed her to the sidelines.

"Listen up, Ashley, and listen good," I said. "Maybe I didn't do a good vault, but I tried. "You're just a coward. You've always got the perfect excuse not to try your hardest."

The Pinecones gathered around me.

I stuck my head down into the huddle. "We can still do it. My score will be thrown out if we all do better. Nobody can foul up." I looked around at each of the faces. "Cindi, Jodi, Lauren, Ti An, and Ashley . . . we're a team. We've got to root for each other."

"But . . . but . . . what if we *can't* do it? What if we all flub our routines like last time?" blubbered Ashley.

"Ashley . . . it's time for you to believe in the Pinecones," I said. "Let's go for it."

The judges flipped the cards to show my score. A 4.3. That was lower than any of the Amazons had gotten and they had all been lousy.

The judges called Ashley's name.

Ashley started for the end of the runway.

"Come on, Ashley!" shouted Cindi. "Go for it!"

"You show them, Ashley," shouted Lauren.

Ashley saluted the judges. She took off. I was holding my breath. She did a great handstand vault, and she nailed her landing.

The Pinecones gave out a huge cheer. Ashley ran back to us. We all gave her a hug.

I watched the girl Hilary bite her fingernails. The Atomic Amazons were being incredibly quiet.

We weren't. We were using the home court advantage. Ti An went next, and she did just as well as Ashley. We were on a roll. Lauren, Jodi, and Cindi nailed their vaults. Every time a Pinecone finished an event, the whole place erupted. I looked over at the audience. GeeGee was leading the cheers by waving her boa.

The judge had to remind the audience to keep quiet during the routines.

But we lost our momentum on the beam, and the Atomic Amazons started racking up the points, just as they had before.

We moved on to the uneven bars. The rip on my palm still hurt a little, but I had taped it up carefully.

Ti An went first. She spent a lot of time chalking up. I knew she was nervous.

"You can do it, Ti An," I said. "You're a fighter."

Ti An squared her tiny shoulders. I was so proud of her. She did the best routine of her life.

The Pinecones were screaming and hollering. Lauren was hugging Ti An.

Ashley went next. She slipped trying to get to the high bar.

"It's okay, Ashley," yelled Cindi. "Think inner door."

Ashley took the full thirty seconds to collect herself. Then she grabbed the lower bar and finished the routine.

It was my turn. I looked up at the doorway. Patrick stood there with his suitcase in his hand.

I saluted the judge and grabbed the lower bar. I swung around, willing myself to forget the pain in my palm. All I thought about was my next move. I felt the rhythm of my swing letting me go higher and higher. I could see myself doing the moves as if I were floating above the uneven bars. I hit the bars so hard that I could hear them creak and crack, but it gave me the momentum.

I really flew on my sole circle dismount.

I barely had time to salute the judges at my finish before I was practically buried under an avalanche of cheering Pinecones.

Patrick bounded over from the sidelines and gave me a hug. "Darlene, that was the best I've ever seen you do."

"We're gonna win," I said, still out of breath. We still had the floor exercise to get through.

Patrick looked up at the scores. "It sure looks like that's what you're going to do," he said.

"Yeah, but we would never have turned it around if it hadn't been for Darlene," said Cindi.

"That's right," said Ashley. "We Pinecones have to help each other."

Patrick looked puzzled. "When did the Pinecones start pulling together?" he asked.

"Our captain knocked our heads together," said Jodi.

112

I blushed. "Well, I just tried to knock some sense into you," I said.

"Whatever it was, it worked," said Patrick.

As the home team it was our responsibility to put together the mats for the floor exercise. I went over to the side where the floor mats were stacked. I could hear Coach Miller yelling at his team. "You're being beaten by a bunch of losers," he said.

Patrick tapped Coach Miller on the shoulder.

Coach Miller looked shocked to see him. "I thought you were fogged in," Coach Miller said.

"You're the one who's fogged in," said Patrick. "Your team is being beaten by a team with more heart and courage than any other."

Coach Miller gave him a dirty look. "They're all just hypnotized by that Grandiose Gladys," said Coach Miller.

"Who's Grandiose Gladys?" asked Patrick.

All the Pinecones started to laugh. It was a great sound, but it wasn't enough. We still had to win.

The judges moved their scoring table over to where they could watch the floor exercise. The Atomic Amazons went first again. None of them scored as high as they had during the first meet. We really did have a chance.

"This is it," I said. The Pinecones gathered

around me. "We've got them in the palm of our hand. We can't stop now."

"Doesn't Grandiose Gladys have a secret plan for us?" joked Lauren.

"Maybe we should have put a whoopee cushion under one of the mats," said Jodi. "That would have shook up the Atomic Amazons."

"No whoopee cushions, no more Grandiose Gladys. This is just the Atomic Amazons against the Pinecones," I said. "We're doing this for Patrick. He told Coach Miller that the Pinecones weren't losers. Well, if we're not losers, we're winners."

"But you can't guarantee that," said Ashley. "We might not win."

"Ashley," I said. "For the last time, shut up. Go out there and be a Pinecone."

Ashley was first up on the floor exercise. I heard the scratchy piano music for "As Time Goes By."

I could barely watch. But through my slitted eyelids I saw Ashley make her aerial cartwheel, and she actually ended her routine in time with the music.

Ti An was the next Pinecone up. She completed her aerial cartwheels beautifully. She rushed the rest of her routine, though, and she finished about ten seconds ahead of the music. Still, she got a high enough score to keep us in the running. Lauren did better. Cindi was next and she did spectacularly. We had pulled to within two points of the Atomic Amazons. I was the last one up on the floor exercise.

I waited for the judges to finish conferring. Coach Miller was standing directly across from the judges, scowling at them.

The Amazons all sat in a perfect row. They were glaring directly at me.

I licked my lips.

I felt Patrick's hand on my shoulder. "Good luck, Darlene," he said. "Give it your all. If you just get a 6.9 we'll win the meet."

"I'm so nervous," I said.

"Did you hear what I said to Coach Miller before?" Patrick asked me.

"You said we weren't losers," I said.

"What else did I say?" asked Patrick.

"That we had a lot of heart."

"We didn't in the first meet," said Patrick. "The Pinecones got that from their captain. You know, Darlene, you were practically a unanimous choice for captain. There was only one vote against you."

I stared at him. I didn't want to tell him that the one vote against me had been mine.

"Go for it, Captain," said Patrick.

The judges looked up and indicated they were ready for me. Ms. Kossuth nodded to me as she got ready to start the music. I walked out onto the mats as if I owned that floor.

I got through the first part of my routine with no mistakes. Now I just had to do my final tumbling pass with the two aerial cartwheels.

My heart was beating so fast that I thought maybe I had too much adrenalin. But sometimes there's just no such thing as too much energy.

I literally flew through the air. I flung myself into my no-handed cartwheel as if I had been doing them without a spot all my life. I had so much energy left after my first one that I practically flung myself into the second one and almost overstepped the mats, but I pulled myself back just in time.

And then as the last notes of "As Time Goes By" played, I finished my routine on the button.

I heard the Pinecones screaming behind me.

I stood up and saluted the judges.

Coach Miller and the Atomic Amazons could do nothing but glare at me. They knew they had lost. Their dirty looks couldn't hurt me.

I waited for my score. 7.3! I ran back to my team.

The Pinecones were jumping up and down for

joy. They practically pummeled me. "Atta girl, Captain!" yelled Cindi. "We're number one!" shouted Jodi, doing a little victory dance. And we were! We are not a cool team. We're the Pinecones, and we're *hot*!

About the Author

Elizabeth Levy decided that the only way she could write about gymnastics was to try it herself. Besides taking classes she is involved with a group of young gymnasts near her home in New York City, and enjoys following their progress.

Elizabeth Levy's other Apple Paperbacks are *A Different Twist, The Computer That Said Steal Me,* and all the other books in THE GYMNASTS series.

She likes visiting schools to give talks and meet her readers. Kids love her presentation's opening. Why? "I start with a cartwheel!" says Levy. "At least I try to."